Chasing Soulmates

Chasing Soulmates

Chasing
Soulmates

Chasing Soulmates

© Copyright 2021 Kathryn Reign

Cover Design by Angela Haddon

Table of Contents

Table of Contents

Table of Contents

Chasing Soulmates

Chapter One: Andrew's Story

"Aw, come on, why do I have to go to this stupid concert, anyway? I thought we were heading to the arcade. The new Star Wars game just came out, and I've been wanting to play since last month," Andrew Cohen complained as he found himself heading toward the Phoenix concert venue in southern downtown Arizona.

The night sky was crisp and clean, the stars were shining bright overhead, and the cool summer night felt breezy against his skin.

Driving straight down Interstate 10, his best friend, Logan Matthews, turned his head slightly. "Sorry, man, maybe next weekend? There's this girl I've been seeing for a few weeks now, and I promised her I'd show up to support her. She's playing tonight, and she'd never let me live it down after I convinced her to sleep with me last week with this promise."

"Really? Another girl? What happened to Amanda? Just last month, you were totally obsessed with her. What the hell happened?"

"Eh, she wasn't really my type, too high-maintenance for me. She always wanted me near her, doing things with her, and it all just became too much. I'm much happier with Cassandra."

Andrew rolled his eyes and sighed. "Cassandra? Who's next? Miranda? Sandra? You going down the whole alphabet?"

"Oh, stop," Logan said as he gave his friend a little push. "You know, you've never really been a fan of any of my girlfriends. Maybe if you stopped playing video games once in a while and start opening yourself up more, you might actually get laid."

"Not everything in life is about sex and girls, Logan. I promised my dad that I'd wait until it was absolutely perfect before I gave myself away. You know that."

"Yeah, and not to be insensitive, but your dad died over twenty years ago. Don't you think it's time to stop holding on and live life the way you want?"

Andrew sighed again, his eyes glazing over the dozens of neon signs pointing toward the concert venue just a couple more miles away. "How many times do I have to tell you? I *am* living life the way I want."

"No, keeping your promise to your dad is only getting you screwed over. I've seen how you behave around girls. You get so nervous that I'm surprised you haven't puked all over them yet."

"What do you mean?"

"You're sheltered, man. You lost the only father-figure in your life, and now you're so afraid of losing another parent that you subconsciously prevent yourself from finding any sort of connection with a woman, afraid she'd steal you away from mommy."

"Hey, dude, cool it. She raised you when yours bailed on you. The least you can do is be respectful."

"Sorry, but you know what I mean. How are you ever going to keep your promise when you can't even talk to a girl for more than five minutes without crapping your pants?"

Andrew remained silent. He knew Logan was right, and he was ashamed of his lack of social skills while his friend seemed to have the charm of ten people. Sure, he gave Logan shit for cycling through girls every month, but secretly, he was jealous, jealous that Logan was able to find love, or whatever he'd call it, so easily.

And he was right, Andrew *was* afraid, afraid of another rejection, just like his mother had done to him right before his father died. She had wanted a baby girl. But when he was born instead, the disappointed look on her face said it all, treating his cousin, Alana, as her own child instead of him.

Andrew reached into his pocket to pull out his wallet. Opening it up, he found a picture of him and his dad, arms wrapped around each other. He struggled to hold back his tears as memories of their last moments together came rushing back to him.

It was a Tuesday afternoon, just him and his dad hanging out at a local arcade and grabbing ice cream afterwards at Pete's Parlor. His favorite was always vanilla while his dad loved his cookie dough. That was one of the best days of his life, yet also one of the worse. The next thing he knew, his dad was lying on the ground at the parlor, clutching his chest and wheezing for air.

"Call 911!" He heard a woman scream, followed by several others rushing toward them.

That was the last time he ever saw his dad alive.

"Hey! Earth to Andrew. Snap out of it. We're here," Logan called over to him, snapping his fingers in his face.

When Andrew looked up, he found himself blinded by even more neon lights, this time, paired with obnoxiously loud music enough to make his head throb. He never did like concerts, or loud noises for that matter. Gave him nothing but migraines. He'd even walked into arcades with headphones on, all just to drown out the sound. People would laugh, but he didn't care.

"Damn it! I can never find any parking in this goddamn place!" Logan yelled in frustration.

Andrew watched as Logan's hands flailed in the air and back down on his steering wheel, circling his car around the many drunk teenagers pre-gaming. "I told you this was a bad idea."

"Oh, shut it, and help me find a spot."

Andrew had known Logan since they were kids, and he always had a temper. When they were five, he threw Andrew's favorite toy robot against the wall and broke it because he didn't have one exactly like it. When they were ten, Andrew swore Logan was reigning hell upon him when he caught a girl he liked staring at Andrew. He always had to get what he wanted.

Even so, Logan wasn't all bad. He had a good heart when he wanted to, and he was always there to protect Andrew from bullies and girls who teased him. He had the anger of a thousand bulls but the heart of an angel toward those he loved.

"There's one!" Andrew shouted and pointed to their right.

There wasn't much space for his SUV, but Logan was determined to make it work. He smashed his foot on the pedal and began speeding up, heading toward the opposite direction of a one-way road.

However, at that moment, another car, coming from the opposite direction, was also making its way to their spot.

"I think that guy's trying to take it." Andrew pointed out.

"Not if I can help it," Logan murmured, disgruntled. He sped up even more, so close to snagging what might be the very last spot in the entire lot. And just when it looked like they were going to make it, the coupe slid in by just a second, Logan slamming on the brakes to keep them from colliding into each other.

"FUCK! Alright, fuck it. I'm parking on the grass. If anyone has a problem with it, they can go kiss my ass."

"What if we get towed?"

"Whatever, there are thousands of people here. No way is anyone even gonna find my car." He turned off the ignition. "And even if they do, I'm too fucking tired to care right now. Come on," he said as he got out of the car. "I gotta find my girl."

Andrew hadn't noticed it earlier, but there was a stark contrast between the way he was dressed and the way Logan was dressed. Dressed in black ripped jeans and a snazzy leather jacket, completed with dark sunglasses, Logan really did outshine him, defending his title as the coolest guy in Phoenix and a ladies' man.

True, he was always the more dapper one, even when he didn't try. But man, when he did, even just a little, he looked like a rock star and the president merged bodies. Compared to him, Andrew's simple plaid button-down over his short-sleeve tee, paired with some dark blue jeans, were nothing to brag about.

His black, thick framed glasses also didn't help. First, they clashed with his thick head of dark hair, his bangs hanging over his eyes and his sideburns dangling over his ears. He definitely didn't have "the look" that Logan always told him many women looked for in a man. He barely even knew how to shop for himself, buying only clothes similar to the ones he had in his closet, clothes his mom had picked out for him.

"Hey, listen man. I gotta go find Cass before she goes on. You know how it is, gotta wish the lady luck. You okay chilling alone?"

Andrew nodded, barely finishing his second nod before Logan disappeared. But he didn't mind. He knew what he was getting into when it came to hanging out with Logan. Women loved him, men wanted to be him, and his ADHD could never make him stand still for longer than fifteen minutes.

Might as well…do something? he thought to himself.

He tried to take a step toward the direction of the stage, but his legs refused to move with him. He just…froze. All the lights, the people, the stench of alcohol and weed, and the blaring music took his anxiety into overdrive, unable to move, and eyes focused on everything, yet nothing, at the same time.

It wasn't until someone knocked into him did reality kick back in.

"Hey, watch it, nerd!" a fat drunken man announced as he burped in Andrew's face and shoved him aside.

Half his size, Andrew was no match, falling over onto the ground in an instant, his glasses falling off his face and onto the grass. Desperate and now partially blind, Andrew felt around him, trying to grab hold of anything hard that could potentially be his glasses.

"Ew! Get off!" He heard a woman scream instead, followed by a sharp kick to the shoulder.

Can't wear those over my eyes.

He rubbed his shoulder and continued to feel around. Despite how loud the music was, nothing was as deafening as the sound of what he heard next, the sound of a loud crack, and his stomach dropped.

"Sorry, it's too dark to see anything around here. Are these yours?" he heard a female voice directed at him.

Awkwardly, he got to his feet and stood up, grabbing his glasses out of the woman's hand and putting it back on his face.

Great.

His left frame had cracked, his headache pounding stronger as a result of the newfound blindness.

When he finally looked up, he had to squint in order to see the woman clearly, adjusting his glasses from the slant it currently sat in.

She giggled and extended her hand again. "Hi, I'm Savannah."

He returned the shake. "Andrew."

"Andrew. I like that name. It's very…sweet."

"Geez, thanks…"

"No! I meant that as a compliment. I like sweet." She smiled at him. He turned away as he found himself glowing red. "So, Andrew, tell me. What brings a guy like you here anyway? You don't seem like someone who's into rock concerts."

"I don't?"

Savannah shook her head. "Look around. Everyone else here looks like they're part of Kiss, and you look like you belong on a farm."

"Hey, what's with the jabs?"

She giggled again. "I'm just messing around. I happen to like what you're wearing. It shows you don't care about fitting in. I admire that."

Andrew smiled. Savannah was one of the most beautiful women he had ever met, her long blonde hair glowing beneath the moonlight as her bright blue eyes glistened at him whenever she smiled.

"What about you? Do you care about fitting in? Your leather jacket and denim skirt sort of says you do."

She blushed, shying away with the turn of her head.

"I'm sorry," Andrew apologized. "I didn't mean to offend you or anything."

She turned her head back toward him. "No, you're right. I do have a tendency of letting others influence me. It's a bad habit I'm trying to break out of."

"Do you like rock concerts? Or did your friends drag you here, too?" he asked, changing the subject.

"They're alright. It's not my favorite thing in the world, but I enjoy them once in a while." She paused. "Your friends dragged you here? Where are they?"

"Just one friend, Logan. He's off chasing some girl. We were supposed to go to the arcade, but he insisted we come here instead. So, here I am, standing here awkwardly and all alone."

"All alone? You have me!" Savannah smiled, tucking a strand of hair behind her ear. "I get it though. I'm not a fan of arcades, but I wouldn't be too excited either if I were you."

"Savannah! Let's go!" Andrew heard another female voice call out right when he opened his mouth to speak.

"Sorry, Andrew, I have to run. It was really nice talking to you. Maybe I'll run into you again." She leaned in closer. "I hope this night gets better for you."

"Thanks."

As Andrew watched Savannah run off toward the stage, a bounce in her steps as she went, he couldn't help but reminisce on how that was the longest conversation he ever had with a girl that actually went pleasantly well.

Chapter Two: Savannah's Story

"Alright, that's a wrap! Thank you everyone for coming out here tonight. We're the Moonshines. And it's been a pleasure, Phoenix!" Savannah Cassidy yelled into her mic before strumming one last time on her guitar and walking back stage.

"Hey, Savannah, I think someone's staring at you," her drummer, Becca Addison, nudged as Savannah went to put her guitar away.

Savanna looked up. "What? Nuh uh, don't be ridiculous."

"No, I actually think she's right. Some cute boy down there," Cassandra chimed in. "Man, if I was still single, I'd totally tap that."

Savannah gave Cassandra a glare. "I'm not single either, remember? I have Frank. Why do you always seem to forget that when you're trying to set me up?"

"Um…maybe because Frank's an asshole? Didn't he pretend like you didn't exist just last week when a pretty girl asked for his number?" Cassandra reminded her.

"Well, I mean, he had a good excuse. It *had* been a long day, and he'd been stressed out about work, and…okay, I guess you're right. But that doesn't mean I'm not still in a relationship." Savannah paused to take a gulp of her water. "Besides, I've been with Frank for so long that I don't think I'll ever move onto someone else. Him and I, we just sort of go together, like peanut butter and jelly."

"Uh, huh, sure." Cassandra rolled her eyes at her. "I'm serious, Cass. I'm not like you. I can't just run off to any guy who flashes a smile in my direction. Who's it now? Lyle? Lucas?"

"Logan," Cassandra corrected.

"Right." Savannah shook her head. "Weren't you just with Ryan? What the hell happened?"

Cassandra shrugged her shoulders, taking a sip of her water. "He went back to his ex."

"Why am I not surprised?" Savannah scoffed.

"What's that supposed to mean?"

"It means, you always fall for the wrong guys, the ones who leave you and break your heart. It's like there's someone new every month. Don't you ever get tired of it?"

"You're the one to talk. Frank literally flirts with girls right in front of you, and you just stand there, powerless. And you're really going to give *me* a lecture?"

Savannah's face began to fume red. She was very well aware that her and Frank had their issues, but whenever someone else brought it up, it amplified them to the point where she struggled to control her frustration. She clenched her fists and gritted her teeth, ready to unleash her feelings. Luckily for the both of them, Becca intervened.

"Hey, hey, break it up, bitches. People are watching. Wait till we get home. Then you can kill each other." Becca spread her arms out, pushing both Savannah and Cassandra further apart.

Savannah huffed. "I need some air."

She propped her guitar case against her other bags and walked off stage, running down the steps while she tried to hold back her tears.

"Hey! Savannah!" She heard someone call out from behind her.

When she turned around, she saw Andrew, smiling and waving at her, his teeth flashing from between his lips.

"Oh, hey," she replied.

He stepped closer to her, but still keeping a respectable distance, and asked, "What's wrong? Is everything okay?"

Savannah sniffled and nodded. She wasn't in the mood to disclose her entire life story to someone she had just met. "It's nothing, just silly drama."

"I'm sorry," Andrew said, looking down at the grass and twisting his toes into the dirt. "I don't really know what those feel like. Pros of being socially awkward, I guess."

That made Savannah smile.

"What?" he asked.

"You're funny, even when you don't try to be. I like that." She looked back over toward the stage. Cassandra was too busy making out with some dude while Becca was nowhere to be seen. "Do you wanna go for…um…a walk with me? Somewhere away from all these people?"

Andrew's eyes opened wider but then dropped back down. "I'd love to, but I should really find my friend. He's my ride, and I wouldn't put it past him to leave me stranded here."

"Come on, please?" she begged. "Just a short walk. You'll be back in no time, I promise."

"Sure." Andrew smiled. "Lead the way."

Savannah gestured her head toward her left, the direction opposite the stage. Andrew nodded and followed suit. As they walked, they passed several dozen concert goers either passed out on the ground or hallucinating that dinosaurs still existed.

The fresh scent of nature had been replaced by beer and body odor, and not a single patch of grass was left unspoiled. The sounds of owls and crickets were nowhere to be heard over the drums of a solo act, and the air was so polluted that not a single star could be seen in the once beautiful night sky.

Andrew finally spoke up after several minutes of walking in silence. "So, you're in a band. I would've never guessed just by looking at you."

"What do you mean?" she asked, looking over at him.

"Well, usually when I picture rock stars, I think wannabes, clout-chasers, you know, those desperate for attention. But when I look at you, I don't imagine you as any of that."

"You figured all that out just by looking at me?"

"I'm pretty good at reading people. My dad used to tell me that what I lack in social skills, I make up for in people perception and empathy. I'm shy, in case you couldn't tell."

Savannah nodded. "Yeah, I sort of figured that out. You don't seem shy around me, though. Why's that?"

Shrugging, Andrew rubbed the back of his neck. "I think…I think, maybe I just feel more comfortable around you. I'm usually afraid to go near people because of what they might say about me, but when we first met, you just seemed so nice, so genuine, that I told myself it might be fine being more open with you."

"Ah, but what if you're wrong?" Savannah asked, flashing Andrew a smirk. "What if I *am* just another one of those no good sleazy, bitchy, rock stars?"

His face dropped, and he froze in his steps. "Are you?" he asked, timid.

Savannah couldn't help but break into a laugh. "Of course not!" Then she paused. "Honestly, I'm not really sure what I am. I haven't really thought about it."

"That's fair. I don't think anyone really has it all figured out. I didn't have a father-figure growing up, and I think living with my mom has made me even more confused than I needed to be."

Savannah stopped walking when they found a tree trunk several yards from the satellite parking lot. She sat down and patted beside her. "Come, sit."

Andrew hesitated. "Uh…I don't think I'll fit."

"Just sit on the opposite side. It'll be fine."

As Andrew eased himself onto the opposite edge, careful to not push Savannah off, she asked, "What happened to your dad?"

"He died," Andrew whispered. "When I was just a kid. From a heart attack, I think. No one ever confirmed it for me. He was my favorite person in the world, and I think about him every day." He paused, then spoke again. "Sorry, I didn't mean to unleash all that on you."

But she didn't shy away. Instead, Savannah placed her hand on top of his, which was resting on top of the trunk. "It's okay," she said. "I get it. Both my parents died when I was seven. I lived with my aunt until I went to college and moved out. Never looked back since."

"I'm sorry," Andrew murmured as he bowed his head down.

"For what?"

"Here I am yammering on about my dad, and you lost both parents. I should be grateful that I still at least have one."

"Are you and your mom close?" Savannah asked, her hand still on top of his.

"We were right after my dad left, but we've drifted apart since. She never wanted me as her own child, and it took years before I finally came to grips with that."

Savannah fell silent, parting the grass by her feet with her shoes. She could relate. Sure, she had the best parents in the world, but living with her aunt had been a nightmare, always bring home disgusting men she met at bars who would try to crawl into bed with Savannah. Her alcoholism and constant smoking didn't help either, and after being kicked out onto the streets, not once, but six times by her aunt who wanted the house to herself, Savannah couldn't be happier to finally move out when she was old enough, flying across the country just to get away from her. Subconsciously, tears began to pool from her eyes.

"What's wrong?" Andrew spoke up after noticing her quietness. "Was it something I said?"

She shook her head.

But that wasn't enough for Andrew to let it go. He stood up, turned himself around, and knelt down beside her. She could tell that his heart was aching just watching her, the empathy in his eyes saying it all. She slightly flinched when he reached up his right hand and brushed aside her tears, starting with one cheek and then moving to the other.

"I can tell you have a lot of pain in your heart, " he said. "And I know we only just met, but I want you to know that if you ever need someone to talk to or just vent or cry to, I can be there for you."

"Thanks," Savannah whispered, wiping her nose with her sleeve.

And before she knew it, she found Andrew's arms wrapped around her. Her mind told her to push him away, the arms of a random guy around her was not something she was used to, but she couldn't. His hug felt so inviting, so warm, instantly melting her tears away.

Instead, she found her own arms wrapping around his back, hands pressed against his shoulders, inching her body closer to his. Everything about this moment just felt so right, like she belonged. Maybe their meeting was fated, or maybe, she just missed the touch of another man. She'd been with Frank for so long that she almost couldn't remember what it felt like to be touched by someone else.

When they finally pulled apart, their arms were still wrapped around each other.

"What was that for?" Savannah asked.

"Human touch always makes people feel better. It looked like you needed one." His eyes twinkled. "Did it work?"

"I think it did."

She sniffled one more time before smiling at him. He returned the gesture. "Good, because I feel much better, too."

A tension washed over them as they continued staring into each other's eyes. Savannah could feel her heart pounding faster, butterflies swarming in her stomach, and her cheeks blushing. Could it be? Could it be that she had feelings toward a man she'd only known for a few hours? Before she could even realize, she found herself leaning in closer to him, their lips almost touching.

"No, sorry," Savannah blurted as she stopped herself and let go. "I…I…I have a boyfriend."

"Boyfriend?"

"Yeah, Frank. We live together, actually."

"Oh," Andrew said.

Savannah felt so guilty and ashamed for even telling him. Andrew had been so nice to her, and she had felt things for someone she never felt before. She wanted nothing more than to leap back over and hug him again, but she couldn't play with him like that, not again. "Is he here with you tonight?"

"Unfortunately, no, he had other plans. I—" Suddenly, her phone rang, interrupting them. She answered it and heard Becca screaming a mile a minute before ending the call. "We should head back."

The walk back to the stage was much quieter than it had been earlier. Savannah hated the strain between them. She hated tension in general, but she couldn't help but feel responsible for hurting Andrew's feelings. He obviously had a crush on her, and she definitely felt things for him, but the timing was just too imperfect.

"Logan! There you are. I've been looking for you," Andrew exclaimed as they found their way back, gesturing toward a man covered in leather with an arm draped around Cassandra.

"Same, man. I am *starving*! I say we bounce and go grab some burgers. But hey, I want you to meet my girl, Cassie." He turned to the girl. "Cassie, this is the guy I've been telling you about, Andrew, my best friend."

"You mean the ner—" Cassandra started to speak.

"And look at you, dude!" Logan interrupted her. "Looks like you found yourself a girl, too! High five, man!"

Savannah knew she should've spoken up, correct everyone and tell them she was already with someone else, but before she could even do so, Becca spoke up for her.

"Uh…no. Savannah already *has* a boyfriend." She turned to Savannah. "Remember Frank? Or did seven years in that relationship just vanish from your mind?"

"Andrew and I are just friends. I'm Savannah," Savannah said to Logan, shaking his hand. "You must be the famous Logan I've been hearing so much about."

Oh, really?" Logan winked. "What else have you heard about me?" he asked, closing the gap between them.

"Logan!" Cassandra interjected, pulling him back to her side.

"I'm just messing around, babe. You know how big my ego gets." He leaned down and kissed her passionately on the lips while the rest of the gang watched in discomfort.

"Ahem!" Becca cleared her throat, breaking the couple apart. "We need to go. I've been up since 6am, and unless you want me to pass out at the wheel, I suggest you swap tongues another time."

"Alright, alright, cool your jets, Becca." He gave Cassandra one last kiss. "We gotta get going anyway. My stomach's calling. Come on, Andrew." He waved and headed toward the main lot.

"B…Bye Savannah. It was really nice meeting you," Andrew said before running off to catch his friend.

Savannah looked onward as they walked away. She couldn't help but wonder if she'd ever see him again. Maybe this was just a chance meeting, or maybe, they were meant to find each other. Andrew was definitely the opposite of Frank, sweet and gentle Andrew. Just yesterday, she thought she was going to marry Frank, spend the rest of her living days with him because that was all she'd ever known. Now, now she wasn't so sure anymore.

Chapter Three: Andrew's Story

The next morning, Andrew woke up with a pounding headache. After stuffing their faces with In-N-Out, Logan convinced him to grab a couple beers at a bar. Andrew had always been a lightweight; even one drink was enough to knock him out.

Groggy, he pulled the sheets off of him and climbed out of bed. He yawned, then reached for his glasses and put them over his eyes before remembering what had happened.

"Oh, great."

He couldn't help but dream about Savannah. Their encounter had seemed so surreal, so unbelievable. Never in his life had he been able to open up to anyone like he did, much less a girl. He didn't know if he was ever going to see her again, the angel who appeared into his life from out of nowhere and took the feelings right out of his heart. Hell, he couldn't even completely recall whether she was real, or whether the smell of weed had just been playing mind tricks with him.

After a quick shower, he threw on a t-shirt and a pair of grey sweatpants, and headed out into the kitchen, where he found Logan crunching on a bowl of Cinnamon Toast Crunch. They had been roommates for the past six years, after Andrew became so fed up with his mom that he forced himself to move out. With nowhere to go and no savings to rely on, he was lucky when he found out that Logan was moving back into town. He'd been deployed in the navy since he was 18, finally retiring when he realized he wanted to pursue something much safer and less hectic, like real estate.

Using the sparse savings he had, he rented out a small apartment in downtown Phoenix and asked

Andrew to move in with him until he could get a job of his own.

Within six months, after nearly two decades of being sheltered by his mother, he finally found his first job working at Staples, at the age of 22. It didn't pay much, and it wasn't his dream job as a video game developer, but the salary was enough to keep him going, and he never had any issues with his boss or coworkers.

"Sup," Logan said, nodding at his sleepy friend walking into the kitchen. "Want some cereal?"

"Huh? Oh, I'm good, thanks. I need to drown myself in coffee. Now."

He rinsed out the carafe and scooped a tablespoon of coffee grounds into a new filter before closing the lid and pressing the button.

Logan chuckled. "I told you not to finish that beer. But you were just sooo determined—"

"I was *trying* not to waste good money," Andrew interrupted. "That beer was eight bucks! No way was I going to just throw that away." He felt a gurgle in his throat. "Excuse me."

He bolted straight to the bathroom, threw his head into the toilet bowl, and gagged, puking up whatever remnants of his burger were still lingering in his stomach.

When he walked back into the kitchen, wiping his mouth on his shirt, Logan gave him a look of disgust. "Shut up," he told him, walking back to his coffee to pour himself a cup.

"Hey, I didn't say a word." Logan defended himself, returning to his cereal. "Grab that toast for me please?" he asked, pointing to the toaster.

Andrew sat down on the chair across from his roommate, tossing the slice of toast on his plate. "Yeah, but you were thinking it." He took a long sip from his mug. "Ah, just what I needed."

"You should really lay off the coffee. It's gonna kill you one day," Logan warned.

Andrew scoffed. "You're one to talk."

"What the fuck is that supposed to mean?"

"Your beer obsession is way worse than my coffee habit. Less than a hundred people die from coffee overdose every year, while alcohol addiction kills several hundred a DAY!"

Logan rolled his eyes. "Alright, whatever, nerd." He grabbed the jar of strawberry jam beside him and spread a thick layer on the toast before folding it in half and shoving the whole thing in his mouth. "So," he said, his word inaudible from his stuffed and sticky mouth. "That girl you were with last night."

"Savannah?"

"Yeah, her. Smoking hot."

"Also, *your* girlfriend's best friend." Andrew reminded him.

Logan held up a finger while he finished swallowing the remnants of his food. "Not my girlfriend. Just hooking up, really. But she's gotten too clingy lately. Not my style, you know? Might get rid of her soon."

"Gentleman of the year," Andrew said, slow clapping sarcastically.

But Logan didn't seem to care. He walked over to the fridge and took a swig from the carton of orange juice.

"How many times have I asked you to stop doing that?" Andrew asked, raising his voice. "Half of that's mine. I don't need to be sucking on your germs."

"I've got the germs of a god," Logan declared, putting the carton back before taking his seat again. He propped his elbows on the kitchen table, inching closer to Andrew. "You hook up with her?"

"What? Of course not!"

"Why not? She's hot, sexy bod, and you've never put your dick in anything, so why not?"

"Because…because she has a boyfriend."

But Logan simply shrugged. "Never stopped me before. Do you like her?"

Andrew paused for a moment. Sure, he liked Savannah, but admitting that would mean opening his heart up to a possibility that could never happen. That would only lead to pain, rejection, and a broken heart. He had liked plenty of girls in the past, each one either rejecting him because of his awkwardness, or simply walking away because of his uncontrollable ability to stare without blinking instead of actually speaking when he needed to.

And Savannah was the cream of the crop. The best of the best. If all the others before her didn't want him, there was absolutely no chance that she would either.

"I…I don't know," he stuttered.

"Then I guess you won't mind if I go after her then."

"No, wait!" Andrew shouted. "Don't."

"Logan smirked, "So, you do like her."

"Not like she's ever going to like me back. I'm a dork, a loser. Even if she *was* single, I'd never have a chance." He reached out and held his mug with both hands, swirling it gently and staring into the dark liquid, sighing.

"Glad you admit it, buddy." Logan patted him on the back as he stood up. "Just be patient, give it time. If it's meant to be, she'll come around."

"Thanks."

"Anytime, bro. Listen, I gotta go meet up with Cass. I won't be back until late. Pizza tonight?"

"Make it a supreme."

Andrew was never much of a socializer. As a kid, he'd spend all his weekends and summers playing video games, and as an adult, that didn't change. Other than Logan, he didn't have any friends. He tried experimenting with online chat rooms once, hoping to meet people he didn't have to physically see, but even then, he had been so paranoid that people were going to find out who he really was and expose him. After that, he never created another account.

But today, he couldn't blow the whole day playing video games like he normally did. He actually had things he needed to get done, well, thing: get new glasses. He wasn't planning on it at first, reasoning with himself that one working lens was still good enough for him. Unfortunately, he didn't plan on falling asleep with his glasses on and crushing the other lens also when he rolled over onto his stomach.

After he made himself some scrambled eggs with cheese and peppers, he went back to his room and got dressed, throwing on a plaid button down and a pair of khakis. He then walked into the bathroom and did a quick combover before rubbing on some deodorant and heading out the door.

One of the perks of living in a big city was that he didn't need a car…which worked out well for Andrew since he didn't even know how to drive. Everything was within walking distance. Phoenix had a versatile public transportation system, and if he did need to go somewhere, Logan had no problem taking him. Things weren't great in Andrew's life, but they were manageable enough where he never found a reason to seek out change.

The optometrist was only a 20-minute walk from his apartment, in the heart of downtown where all the shops and restaurants were located and where all the tourists gathered for the infamous Arizona nightlife. He could never understand the fascination people had with large crowds and sticky streets. There were too many cons with not enough pros that made Andrew stay as far away as he could from it whenever possible. Logan, on the other hand, found himself smacked in the center every night.

"I won't stop even when I'm 80." He once told him.

When he reached the front door of the office, his phone rang. He fished it out from his pocket and looked at it. It was a number he didn't recognize but decided to answer it anyway.

"Hello?"

"Andrew?" the voice on the other line asked.

"Yes?"

"Andrew, it's me, Savannah. From the concert?"

A smile slowly pasted over Andrew's face. He never thought he'd hear from her again, and the sound of her voice made his heart skip a beat.

"Hey, Savannah. It's good to hear from you…how'd you get my number? Was I so out of it last night that I gave it to you but just don't remember?"

She giggled. "I got it from Cass. She helped me ask Logan for it."

Andrew's heart skipped a beat again. Could it be that she may actually be interested in him? Why else would she be asking around for his number? Maybe he really did have a chance. Maybe their meeting really was fate.

He wanted nothing more than to spill out his feelings, to confess to her how he felt, but he knew that would only scare her away. "What's up?" he asked, clearing his throat.

"Do you want to go grab some coffee with me? There's something I want to talk to you about."

Andrew still felt shaky from his three cups that morning. As much as he loved the fix, he knew he shouldn't down another one. But this was his chance to hang out with Savannah, be around her again. He'd force himself to down ten cups if he had to. "Su…sure, of course. I have to get new glasses, but we can meet up around noon."

"Oh, no! Your glasses! I'm so sorry again for stepping on one of the lenses."

He laughed. "It's fine. I slept on them and broke the other. I guess we're both clumsy."

"Fair enough." She giggled again. "See you at noon. I'll text you the address."

When Savannah hung up, Andrew immediately saved her number, typing in her name slowly and carefully. He didn't want to risk making any mistakes that would cause him to have the wrong number. Everything needed to be just right.

Ten minutes before noon, the text from Savannah popped up. Macchiaddiction was the name of the coffee shop, one of the older coffee shops in the southern downtown area.

Ever since the neighborhood began gentrifying, more and more cafés had been popping up, hipster, vegan, fast-paced places that had taken over honest mom and pop shops like Macchiaddiction. And Andrew liked that Savannah had chosen it. It was one of his favorite places to get his weekly Saturday morning caramel macchiato.

When he arrived, his presence triggering the bell above the door, it didn't take him long to spot

Savannah, who waved at him as he walked in. She had changed out of her leather and denim look and substituted it for a more modest floral dress. Her blonde curls were draped over her shoulders, and the gloss on her lips shined in the sunlight as she sipped on her iced coffee.

"Hey, Andrew." She smiled when she looked up. "I'm so glad you came."

"My pleasure. I'm glad you called." He looked around. The place was completely empty aside from them and the old lady working behind the counter. "Okay, I need to ask. Of all the places, why'd you choose this place?"

A look of concern washed over Savannah's face. "Why? Do you not like it? We can go somewhere else if you want."

She reached for her bag, but he stopped her in her reach. "No, no, no, sorry, I was just curious." "I don't know," she said, shrugging her shoulders. "I just like it here. It's quiet. Away from people. Cares more about quality than flashiness. I like the quiet." She caught Andrew staring intensely at her. "What? Why are you looking at me like that?"

He shook his head, shaking away his thoughts. "Sor...sorry, I didn't mean to be creepy. It's just that...well, I've never heard anyone else say that.

Everyone around here loves the trendy restaurants and hip shops. I've never met anyone else who preferred calmer, slower places like this." He paused. "This is my favorite coffee shop. I'm glad you picked it."

She smiled at him. "Favorite, huh? I guess that means you're an expert then. So, tell me, Andrew. As a first-timer here, what do you recommend? Blow my mind with the BEST thing this place has to offer."

"Hmm." He rubbed his chin with his fingers as he contemplated. He was definitely up for the challenge and was excited to share with Savannah what he loved. "I say, the French Vanilla Cappuccino and the Frosted Lemon Square. You haven't experienced happiness until you've experienced those two together."

"Ooo, sounds delicious. I guess I know what I want."

"I promise you won't regret it. Wait here, I'll be right back."

As Andrew walked up to the counter to order, he couldn't help but notice Savannah staring at him, her elbows on the table and her chin propped atop her hands. He felt himself blushing and turned his head back.

"Hey, Ms. Madge, how's it going today?"

"Oh, not bad, Andy. Business has been a bit slow lately, but it's good, loyal customers like you that keep us going. So, what's it going to be today? Another caramel macchiato?" she asked.

Andrew chuckled. "Nope, those are my special Saturday treat. Can I get two small French Vanilla Cappuccinos and two of your famous Frosted Lemon Squares, please?"

Ms. Madge glanced over to Andrew's left and caught a glimpse of Savannah, adjusting her glasses when she returned. "Is that what I think it is? Did you finally get a girlfriend?"

Andrew blushed, then shook his head. "I wish; she's just a friend."

"Well, maybe after she tries this lemon square, she'll change her mind. It is an aphrodisiac, after all."

"Ha-ha, we'll just have to see."

When Andrew sat back down with their tray of food, Savannah was quick to whip out her wallet.

"How much do I owe you?" she asked.

"What? No, don't worry about it. It's on me."

"Are you sure?"

"Positive."

She gave him a weak grin, almost as if she felt guilty, and put her wallet back in her bag. "Wow, this looks freaking amazing!" she exclaimed, looking down at the tray. She then pointed at one of the lemon squares. "How are these glistening like this?" she asked.

"Heh, Ms. Madge has been doing some sort of sorcery back there since 1992. Now, you know why I come here so often. Pure perfection!" He picked off a piece of the dessert closest to him and popped it into his mouth. "So, what did you want to talk to me about?"

Savannah's face instantly fell. "Oh, right."

"Is everything okay?"

"Yeah, yeah, fine. It's just a little hard to talk about, that's all." She took a sip of her cappuccino. "Wow!"

"Right?" Andrew asked, nodding in agreement. He then reached his right hand across the table and placed it on top of hers. "Hey, Savannah, you know you can tell me anything, right? I won't judge. I promise."

She sighed and wrapped her slender fingers around his hand. "With your heart and soul?"

"With every organ I have in my body."

She giggled, and then her face turned serious again. "I broke up with Frank."

Andrew's heart started beating faster, and he struggled to force himself not to smile. "What happened? Are you okay?"

Savannah nodded. "Things have been pretty rough for a while now. And I hate that it took me this long to realize it."

Andrew listened patiently as Savannah spilled her heart out about how her relationship with Frank went sour just only after a few months in, starting from arguments and then extending to physical and emotional abuse.

"I don't know why I couldn't see it sooner, why I couldn't see how bad he was for me. All these years, wasted on someone who couldn't stop looking at other women long enough to notice me." Tears began to heavily flow from her eyes. "It wasn't until I met you. I just knew I had to end it. One phone call last night, and just like that, it's over. The worst part is, I don't even think he cared."

"I'm so sorry, Savannah. I swear, I didn't mean to break up your relationship. I don't even remember doing anything."

"You didn't."

"I'm confused."

Savannah finished her drink and stood up. Andrew braced himself, expecting her to walk out the door and out of his life forever. But instead, she moved over to his side and sat beside him, this time, taking *his* hand in hers.

"Andrew, meeting you last night made me feel things I haven't felt in a while. You're so easy to talk to, and I felt myself connected to you, like our stars just aligned. You made me feel…well, like me, like I didn't have to pretend." She gripped his hand harder and inched closer to him, their hips touching side by side. "I like you, Andrew."

Grinning from ear to ear, he placed his other hand on top of their conjoined grasps. "I like you too, Savannah."

"I know this might be weird to ask, but…" Savannah started to speak.

"…Will you be my girlfriend?" Andrew finished, his mind failing to register his words until they were out of his mouth.

Eyes wide and glistening, Savannah wrapped her arms around his neck and teared up with happiness. Andrew wrapped his own arms around her back, pulling her close to him, and stared in awe while Ms. Madge gave him a thumbs up. Was this really happening?

Chapter Four: Andrew's Story

After their meeting at Macchiaddiction, Andrew and Savannah hung out every day. Surprisingly, they both enjoyed similar things, from mini-golf to parks to the movies, anywhere that spared them the ruse of intoxicated drunks and blasting music.

Their relationship was slow and innocent, and although Andrew didn't know how to take it any other way, he knew Savannah preferred it that way.

This was Andrew's first experience dating anyone, in the twenty-something odd years of his life. Before this, the extent of his relationships centered around anime girls he fantasized over and video game characters, but never someone real.

And Logan couldn't be more thrilled for him.

"So proud of you, man, so proud." Tears welled in his eyes when Andrew told him for the first time. "Still kinda pissed that your girl is hotter than mine though, but I forgive you. My little man is finally all grown up!" He pulled Andrew into a bro hug and patted him on the back. Then he pulled back and asked the question Andrew never wanted to hear from anyone. "When you gonna give her the D?"

"Dude, shhh, stop!" Andrew said, flustered.

"What? Why you shushing me? There's no one else here, and you know damn well that you can't hide your virginity from me. We're bros, remember? I know everything about you, everything down to your dick size."

"Yeah…" Andrew started. "Wait, what?"

Logan looked down. "Your shoes. Pretty obvious what you got packing in there."

"Look, I'm just…I'm just not ready, okay? I'm not ready to tell Savannah my secret. It's too embarrassing. She'll laugh at me."

"Maybe, but maybe not," Logan contemplated, rubbing his chin. "But you gotta tell her soon enough. Else you want her to leave you."

"I know. Trust me, I know."

Head down in defeat, Andrew grabbed a can of root beer from the fridge and headed to his room. Savannah was spending the whole day preparing for her concert tomorrow, so Andrew decided to spend his day online gaming. He knew Savannah had enough stress from Becca and Cassandra alone, and he didn't want to add to it.

"Maybe we can hang out after," she offered.

But Andrew knew it would've been a bad idea. She needed her sleep, and with so many people watching her, he didn't want to be the reason for her missing her solo.

He placed his can on his desk, turning on his computer, and within seconds, a chat popped up on his screen.

V: Hey, Andrew. How's it hanging?

That left him confused. He hadn't spoken to anyone on his stream in years. The sheer potential embarrassment was all too real for him to handle. He struggled to remember who this person was, and whether he should even answer.

Hey, he ended up typing back. Um…who's this?

V: Who's this? Who's this?! It's me, Vanessa! Don't you remember? From our Zelda days?

His memory began to jog slightly. He remembered Vanessa. They met online six years ago when he dabbled with online gaming, thinking it would be fun to have real people on his team for once. Vanessa was one of them. But the extent of their conversation only lasted three days, before Andrew ultimately decided it wasn't for him. He couldn't keep up with the constant chatting going back and forth. It distracted him from the game and gave him anxiety whenever he felt forced to answer someone back. How she even remembered him, or why she decided to reach out, was beyond him.

A: Oh, yeah, hi.

V: So, how's everything going? Still trying to defeat Ganon? Last time, you were so insistent on it that I thought you were just gonna reach through your screen and strangle him with your bare hands.

A: Oh, him? Killed him years ago. Wasn't too bad.

V: Lol. Anyway, you're probs wondering why I'm reaching out, you know, after all these years.

A: Yeah, sort of.

V: Last time we spoke, you mentioned that you live in Phoenix.

A: Yeah...?

V: Do you still?

A: Yeah…? Why?

V: Well, surprise! I'm visiting the Grand Canyon with my family and since it's only a couple hours away, I was wondering if you'd wanna meet up, see each other for real instead of through avatars.

Andrew swallowed a lump in his throat. *Meet up in person?* His social anxiety kicked into overdrive, and he wanted nothing more than to hide in his closet.

A: I dunno. Not really my thing.

V: Oh, come on, please! I really liked playing with you, and when you just stopped joining our chat rooms, I was devastated. You were one of my favorite people on there.

A: I am kinda busy, and…

V: Just one meetup. I promise. I'm heading back to New York in two days anyway, and if you hate it, I'll never ask you for anything ever again. In fact, I'll even let you block me completely. Deal?

Andrew paused again to think. He was never good at saying no to people, and his introversion had done a great job of driving any potential friends away to date, but maybe it wouldn't be such a bad idea to have another friend in his life, to stop being such a loser, as Logan would put it.

Alright, fine, he finally conceded. One meetup.

V: Sweet! See ya tomorrow!

***

The next morning, Andrew found himself sweating as he pulled his sweater over his head for his meeting with Vanessa. He didn't know what to expect, whether Vanessa was even Vanessa, whether this person was a serial killer.

Several times that morning, he contemplated backing out, to just ghost her without saying anything and block her forever. But deep down, he knew he couldn't. A promise was a promise. And he had never been one to go back on his word.

He checked his watch as he knotted his shoes.

11am. Good, he thought.

Savannah was playing at the Roxbury later that night, and he had to make sure he left ample time to bring her favorite pre-concert treat, strawberry crème ice cream, before she went on stage. It was a ritual she had before every show, and after they began dating, Andrew vowed to her that he would make sure she had that in her hands at all times.

He checked his phone as he came to a stop at a red brick building to make sure he had the right place. He could smell the delicious aroma of brick-oven pizza soaring into his nose, and when he walked inside, his stomach rumbled.

Unfortunately for him, the stomachs of dozens of others were also rumbling, and Andrew shivered at the thought of having to figure out who Vanessa was in this massive crowd.

He checked his phone again to read what she had sent.

Hey, Andrew. I'm sitting by the back window. Purple top, black hair, black jeans, shit ton of golden bangles. Can't miss me.

It didn't take him long to see her when he figured out where to look. There she was, exactly as described. Her hair was long, and her face was plastered in makeup, with dark eyeshadow and bright red lipstick. She definitely wasn't the pimply redhead gamer he had expected.

"Um…Vanessa?" he asked, standing in front of her.

She looked up. "Andrew? Hi!" She stood up and gave him a long hug. "I'm so glad we finally get to meet!"

"Me too." He took a seat across from her.

"Hey! I'm starving. Do you wanna order some pizza? I hear it's bomb here!"

Andrew nodded.

"Sweet! I'm thinking a large sausage with extra cheese? Sound good?"

"Sure."

Andrew watched, his hands still shaking, as Vanessa called the waiter over and placed their order. She was so extroverted, such a people's person, the complete opposite of him. He'd always thought that all gamers were shy, just like him, but she was just so different from what he'd imagined.

"I gotta say, Andrew. You look *nothing* like how I imagined you to be." She propped her elbows on the table and took a long sip of her iced water. "Ah, nothing like a refreshing glass of freezing cold water in the beating heat of Arizona."

Andrew chuckled quietly. "Yeah," he agreed. "It gets pretty rough here. What did you imagine me looking like?"

Vanessa shrugged. "Oh, I dunno, maybe greasy, overweight, balding, something along those lines."

"Really? Were your expectations really that low?"

She laughed out loud. "No, I'm just joking!"

"No, you're not."

"Okay, fine, no I'm not. But I'm glad I was wrong. To be honest though, you *are* kinda hot for a gamer."

Andrew's cheeks turned red; his head turned slightly away. "I am?"

"Pssh, are you kidding? Of course! If I saw you on the street, I'd never peg that you were into Dungeons and Dragons."

They spent the next several hours immersed in conversation, digging into their pizza while discussing their favorite games and RPGs. Vanessa was actually pretty cool. First Savannah, and now Vanessa, maybe he was actually doing something right for once in his life. Maybe his luck had changed when it came to meeting new people.

But she was no Savannah. In his mind, no one could replace Savannah. He had connected with her so well, and even felt like he was falling in love with her, that he didn't think anyone could come close to ever replacing that.

"Hmm, this pizza is so fucking good!" Vanessa exclaimed, wolfing down her third slice. "Tell me, what are your thoughts on horror?"

"Oh, you mean like Doom? They're okay. They sort of scare me sometimes. I'm more into quests and adventure."

"Same!" She took another bite before putting the rest down on her plate. She then reached out to touch Andrew's hand. He shivered. "You know, Andrew, I *was* a bit nervous about meeting you at first, but I'm glad I did. You're a really cool dude, and we have so much in common."

"Yeah, I guess." He slowly pulled his hand back, his body uncomfortable by the touch of another woman.

"And I'd love to get to know you more. Swap numbers?"

Without thinking more into it, Andrew agreed. When he reached into his pocket to pull out his phone and put her digits in, he caught sight of the time.

"Shit!" he yelled.

Startled, Vanessa looked up after entering his in. "What's wrong?"

"Shit! I'm late. I have to go." He reached into his pocket and pulled out a twenty. "For the pizza. Sorry, but I really gotta go."

Without even waiting for her to answer, he shoved his phone back into his pocket and bolted out the door, dashing down Washington Street and praying that Savannah would forgive him.

Chapter Five: Andrew & Savannah's Story

"Hey, Savannah, so sorry I'm late. I meant to come sooner, but the store I went to didn't have the flavor you wanted, and I know how much you love strawberry crème so I had to try three other places before I could finally find it," Andrew panted as he rushed inside the venue, pulling his soaked hood off his head, his dark strands twinkling beneath the light.

Savannah opened her mouth, but before she could say a word, Becca ran in between them and began to yell, "Sorry? Sorry? Are you kidding me, dude? You barely made it back in time. Savannah's up in less than five minutes, and you're dripping all over my freshly-polished floor! I knew all along that you weren't good for her. I fucking knew it."

"Hey, Becca, lay off. I got this. Just start setting everything up," Savannah insisted to Becca as she pointed toward the stage. She turned back to Andrew. "Andrew, I…"

"Wait, before you say anything else, Savannah, please know that I really wanted to come sooner and support you with your favorite pre-performance treat. I really did. I know how much it means to you. I'm really, really sorry. I just wish…"

Savannah placed a finger over his lips, stopping him in his speech. "Andrew, it's okay, really. I understand. I understand how hard you tried. You're soaking wet, and you look more stressed out than me, and I'm always sweating bullets before a show." She grabbed the bag from his hands. "I'm going to have to eat this later, but I can't wait to dig in. Thank you for finding this. In all honesty though, I would've settled for chocolate." She giggled, a smile forming across her face.

Seeing Savannah smile always made him smile back. For the longest minute, they both stood there, gazing into each other's eyes. Savannah leaned in closer, wrapped her arms around Andrew's neck, and pulled him in for a kiss. His first kiss. Andrew didn't know how to respond. He had never been intimate with anyone before, but his body kept pushing him to wrap his arms around her waist and pull her in even closer. He kissed her back, the warmth of his lips sending tingling shivers throughout his body, and he pulled her in closer again.

Out of the corner of her eye, Savannah could see Becca glaring daggers at her. Becca had recently gotten out of a relationship, and Savannah was sure she wanted everyone else to feel as miserable as she was feeling. But she didn't care. She was enjoying her kiss with Andrew. His lips were so soft and tender, his tongue adventurous but gentle, and the way he wrapped his arms around her body was worth more to her than all her past relationships combined.

When they finally pulled away, Savannah lowered her head while Andrew grazed her left cheek with his hand. She grabbed onto his arm and whispered, "Andrew, I'm in love with you. I know I shouldn't be saying this because I'm flying back home in a week, and all this will just fall apart like it never happened, but you're the most amazing guy I've ever met, and I love you. Please don't hate me for saying that. I know this was just supposed to be for fun."

Savannah could tell by the fallen look on Andrew's face that he was shocked by her news. She never really told him where she actually lived, and she never thought they'd have to cross that bridge when they started dating.

"Home? Back?" he asked.

She nodded, ashamed. "I live in Portland."

"Oregon? That's not *too* far from here. Maybe we can still—"

"Maine," she corrected him, her heart breaking from the look of disappointment on his face.

However, instead of the scorn or anger Savannah was expecting, she was met a smile and hopeful eyes. "I love you too, Savannah. God, I've been wanting to say something ever since we went on our first date. I couldn't stop thinking about you. And I knew I didn't want to stress you out by bringing unnecessary drama into your life, but I've loved you since I first saw you." He reached out his other arm and pulled Savannah into a hug. "I can't explain it, but I feel it in my heart that we're meant to be together. I know we can make this work. I just know it."

"I…" Savannah started to speak.

"Savannah, hurry up! We're starting." Becca yelled from the stage.

"I have to go. I'll call you later," she blurted, pulling her arm in the opposite direction but found herself stuck when Andrew held her back.

"One more for good luck." He spun her back around, wrapped his right hand around the back of her head and gave her the most passionate kiss she had ever experienced. She could tell that he really wanted her, that he wanted more than just casual hand holding and friendly hugs. He wanted more.

Her hands found their way under his jacket, under his sweater, and onto his bare back. He trembled slightly but continued to massage her lips with his. She felt herself living in pure ecstasy, until her wandering mind was brought back by another interruption of Becca's screaming voice.

Hesitantly, she pulled away. "I wish I could do this all night, but I really have to go. Find me after the show, okay?"

"Definitely." His eyes twinkled beneath the blue fluorescent light. "I love you so much, Savannah."

"I love you too, Andrew."

When the concert was over, Andrew went around back to find Savannah. However, to his surprise, he found her surrounded by teenage boys with hungry eyes. They all leered at her like she was a piece of meat, eyes darting toward her cleavage while she signed their CDs. His body dripped with sweat, and the vessels behind his eyes felt like they were going to explode out through his eyes. He wanted nothing more than to walk up to each and every one of them, and clock them in the face.

Out of the corner of her eye, Savannah noticed Andrew lingering nervously by the edge of the stage, away from all the eager fans. She excused herself from the crowd and walked over to him.

"Hey, sweetie. Did you like my show?" She wrapped her arms around his neck and pecked him on the lips.

"Sure," he murmured, his eyes focused on his shoes as he rubbed the toes of one side on top of the other.

"Hey, I know that look. I know when something's bothering you. What's wrong?" She reached out and touched his arm; his body was stiff and unmoving.

"It's just…all these guys. They're all over you. And it also doesn't help that your…your…things are practically hanging out."

"You mean boobs?"

"Yeah, those."

"Are you jealous? Andrew, sweetie, they're VIP. They paid extra to get the chance to meet us. It's just an autograph signing. Innocent." She grabbed both his arms and turned him to face her. "They mean *nothing* to me. It's you I love, remember? You."

Andrew relaxed his body slightly, but he still felt flustered. "Yeah, but I saw them look—"

"No buts," she interrupted him. "You, I love you." She grabbed his face and pulled it down toward hers, locking their lips and encircling their tongues before pulling away. "There, see? If I was interested in my fans, would I kiss you in front of them?"

"I guess not…"

"Okay, then, now let me go finish up a few more, and we can get out of here. I'm DYING to dig into my ice cream. I've been craving it all night."

❋❋❋

Several hours later, Andrew and Savannah found themselves sitting on his couch and watching a movie while Savannah scooped a spoonful into her mouth. Logan had gone out with Cassandra after the concert, so they had the whole apartment to themselves. Savannah stripped off her jacket, exposing the cropped tank top and short skirt she had underneath, and tucked her bare feet beneath her as she snuggled up beside Andrew.

"Bite?" she asked, holding up a spoonful of ice cream to his mouth.

He grinned at her and opened his mouth to accept it. "Wow, you're right! This really is a treat."

She laughed. "Wait, don't tell me you've never had ice cream before!"

"Not since I was a kid. I'm not really a fan of cold things, but it's nice to enjoy them every now and then."

"Is that why you live in Arizo—"

He looked over. "Everything okay?"

"Huh? Oh, yeah, I'm just a little sad that I have to fly home soon. What's going to happen to us? Does that mean we have to break up?" She started sniffling, sadness overwhelming her eyes as she choked on her dessert.

"Hey, hey, hey, it's okay. I'm still here. I'm right here." He gently rubbed her cheeks and pushed her blonde hair out of her face. "We'll make this work, I promise. Even if I have to fly to you every weekend. I swear to you. I'm not letting you go."

"That's…that's so hard though! You're going to get tired eventually, and then you'll stop coming. Soon enough, you'll just move on to someone else, someone who's closer."

"No, I won't. I swear." He kissed her forehead, then each cheek, before coming down to her lips. "You're literally the best thing that's ever happened to me. If I were to let you go now, because of something as stupid as distance, I'd be the dumbest guy on Earth. I love you, Savannah."

She stared into his eyes and then pulled out her pinky finger. "Pinky swear?"

"Pinky swear? I haven't done that since I was five."

"Come on! Pinky swear that we'll never break up. Come on, do it!"

"Alright, alright! Fine, pinky swear." He whipped out his own pinky and intertwined it with hers.

They held their position for a moment, refusing to look away from each other. Before he knew it, he found her lunging at him and climbing on top of him, her slim bare legs on either side of his waist and her body sitting on top of his. He didn't know what was happening at first, his inexperience confusing innocence and lust. It wasn't until she started ripping off his clothes that he was forced to stop her.

"Wait," he said.

"What's wrong?"

"I…I…I'm not sure if I can do this," he stuttered, still holding onto her waist.

The hurt expression on her face pained him as her face fell. "Oh my god, is it me? Do you not want me?"

"No, no! I do! I really, really do. You're sexy, beautiful, and I've been dreaming about this day for weeks. It's just that…" He turned his head away, his cheeks turning red. "It's just that I've…never done this before."

"What do you mean?"

"I'm a virgin."

He braced himself, expecting her to burst out into laughter, his biggest fear realized. He expected her to be like Logan, who would taunt him every year for still being single and unlaid. He winced, expecting the worse, but when nothing happened, he opened his eyes again and found Savannah giving him a compassionate look.

"Are you mad?" he asked, "That I'm not experienced?"

She shook her head. "Of course not. In fact, that makes me love you even more. You're pure, untouched, all mine. Like you were saving yourself for me all along. I'm sorry I can't be the same for you, but Andrew," she said, taking his hand, "I don't care that you've never had sex. Do you know why?"

"Why?"

"Because now, I can be the one to show you."

He felt his heart pounding a million miles a minute, his breath heaving faster and faster. She turned the left corner of her mouth up and picked up his hand, placing it over her heart.

"Do you feel this? This means I'm yours, forever." She then leaned him over on the couch again, climbing back over him, this time, slower and gentler. "I want to be your first love," she whispered.

She reached toward her chest and unzipped her top, letting it fall over her shoulders as she exposed her black bra, her hands then reaching down toward her waist and caressing Andrew's crotch.

The intensity grew stronger and stronger for Andrew, droplets of sweat appearing on the back of his neck and his forehead when he found his hormones raging angrily, and he couldn't hold himself back any longer. He grabbed her by the shoulders and pulled her down, entangling his tongue with hers again before moving his lips down to her neck, smelling her perfume and tasting her as she moaned and leaned closer over him.

"Oh, Andrew, please don't stop."

He continued moving down, down her collarbone, over her shoulders, and closing in on her chest. He came to a stop and stared at the cleavage over her bra. "May I?" he asked.

When she nodded, he reached around her and found his fingers toggling the clasp. It didn't take long before he figured it out, and when he removed her bra, his jaw dropped. He had seen pornography before, but none of the porn stars even came close to the immaculate wonder of Savannah.

"They're beautiful," he whispered, leaning his face closer to them and circling each nipple like he was hungry for her.

They found themselves in that position for the next ten minutes. Savannah grinding her hips over his crotch, the warmth causing him to rise while her hand made its way down into his pants and stroked him to erection. Andrew's hands roamed from her back to her waist, and eventually further down and massaging her cheeks. He felt his entire life passing him, his mind in such hedonistic pleasure that he couldn't focus on anything else.

"I want to feel you inside me," Savannah whispered into his ear.

But before Andrew could say another word, he knew that she would be taking charge. "Shh." She placed a finger over his lips. "Just relax."

She got on her knees and removed the rest of her clothing, undoing the Velcro holding her skirt together and untying the strings securing her thong. Completely naked, Andrew stared in awe. He still couldn't believe what was happening. Everything felt so unreal, from the moment he met Savannah, to the moment they first kissed, to this, he was about to lose his virginity to the woman of his dreams.

She climbed over him one more time, this time, undressing him. He felt so vulnerable. He'd always been insecure about his body and feared the day when a girl would finally see him and judge him. But Savannah didn't seem to care. She stared at him like she was unwrapping a present, and soon enough, they connected, like two pieces of a perfect puzzle, and their naked bodies pressed against each other like they belonged.

"I love you," he said again, his eyes rolling back in pleasure as Savannah rocked her body faster and faster on top of his.

"Shut up, and kiss me."

Chapter Six: Logan's Story

"See you again tomorrow night?" Ava asked Logan after she pulled her dress over her head and slipped on her heels.

"We'll see," he responded, indifferent as he yawned into his hand.

"Aw, come on, Logan. We had such a great time last night." She inched closer. "I'll let you play out your fantasy." She winked.

He thought about it for a minute before ushering her out the door. "Maybe. I'll call you."

She turned around and blew him a kiss. "You better, handsome."

"One of these days, Cassandra is gonna find out."

Logan spun around, startled by the voice. "Oh, it's just you. Nah, she'll never know. I've been doing this for years. Never been caught once. Gotta tell ya though, definitely keeping me on my toes."

"Still don't approve." Andrew shook his head and reached for the box of Frosted Flakes.

"What? You gonna narc to your girl? Sell me out?"

"Don't be ridiculous! I would never do that." He poured himself a bowl, topping it off with some 2% milk, and took a bite. "Doesn't mean I can't still judge you for it."

"And that's something I can live with." He pulled open the cabinet behind him and grabbed a packet of strawberry-frosted Pop-Tarts before sitting down in front of Andrew. "How's it going with Savannah, anyway? Still bummed that she's leaving soon?" He unwrapped the packaging and took a bite.

"That's your breakfast?"

"What, and you really think your cavity-filled cereal is any better?"

"Fair enough," Andrew conceded, shrugging his shoulders. "I don't know, Logan. I keep getting these nagging thoughts that something bad is going to happen when she leaves. What if she gets back together with Frank? What if she leaves me for one of her fans? I saw how much they were all over her. With nearly three thousand miles between us, there's no way we stand a chance."

Taking another bite, Logan said, "You never know. Stranger things have happened in our crazy, messed-up world. Maybe one day, I'll even stop having so many side chicks."

"You? I don't think that's ever happening."

"Ha-ha, listen, man, gotta run for a hot date. I probably won't be home for dinner. You cool with that?"

Andrew simply rolled his eyes and said, "Again?"

"I know, I know, but Ashley's super sexy. Met her last week at the concert."

"Don't you feel bad for what you're doing to Cassandra? She worships you like a king, and here you are, screwing around with everything with boobs."

"Hey, when my conscience starts to get the best of me, I'll know. Until then, I feel nothing."

He shoved the rest of the Pop-Tarts into his mouth before crumbling up the wrapper and tossing it at

Andrew. He then grabbed his wallet and car keys, and headed out the door.

As he drove toward the west side of town, where Ashley lived, his phone sounded. He looked over at the dashboard where he had propped it and saw a text from Cass.

Hey, Logan. I miss you! When can I see you again?

Sighing, he reached over and cleared the message. He had enough going on already, from his lecture from Andrew to the constant calls from Ava. He didn't need yet another thing on his plate ruining his day with Ashley.

The text was soon followed by a call, but Logan screened it, turned his phone off, and continued driving.

When he finally reached Glendale, he made his way through the winding neighborhoods to the address he was given. When he turned the corner, he found himself staring at a small cottage home, something rare to find smacked in the middle of a desert. He parked his car by the curb and stepped out, his white t-shirt and basketball shorts cooling him off from the searing heat beating down on his shoulders.

"Hey! Back here!" He heard a woman shout.

He swung his body around and saw Ashley in the thinnest bikini he had ever seen. The top was barely enough to cover her double Ds, and the bottom left no room for imagination. He felt his pants getting tighter as he tried to keep his composure and walked around back to the yard.

"I'm glad you came," she said as she gave him a seductive look. "I didn't think I'd hear from you after that night." She walked closer to him, placing her hands on his chest, and whispered into his ear. "I never forgot about that kiss."

Logan quivered when she kissed the side of his face, running her tongue down to his lips before inserting it into his mouth. A surprise to him, part of him tried to resist, the guilt from what he was doing overwhelming his natural instincts. But when she pressed her body up against him, those thoughts instantly disappeared, and he wrapped his hands around her back, pulling her closer to him.

Moments later, she pulled away and gestured him into the pool. She stepped in first, the translucent water splashing through her silky skin, and her hair flowing freely over the clear water waves. She looked nothing less than an angel, a beautiful angel that he couldn't wait to ravage and take as his.

Frantically, he stripped himself down to nothing but his boxers and jumped in after her, grabbing her by the waist again and kissing her.

"So, who's that girl that was all over you at the concert?" she asked, letting her body float lightly beside him.

"Girl?"

"You know, the mousy-looking one with brown hair." She paused for a moment. "Actually, I think she might've been the bassist."

A look of guilt glazed over his face, but he quickly washed it away. "Oh, her? Nobody. I was just getting to know the band a bit. Music just speaks to me sometimes. I'm very eclectic like that."

"Honorable." She nodded. "I respect that."

"Anyway." He turned to face her and pulled her against him, their wet bodies touching. He could feel the mini triangles of her bikini top slowly beginning to slide off as their chests rubbed together. "I didn't come all the way out here just to talk." He reached around back and undid the knot, running his lips up and down her neck and eventually across her chest.

"Logan?" He heard faintly in the background. At first, he passed it off as Ashley moaning his name, for him to keep going. So, he did, moving his lips further and further down, until he heard it again.

"Logan!"

He moved his head back up and looked over at Ashley. Her eyes remained closed and her body in heat that it couldn't have been her.

"Logan!"

He whipped his head to look behind him.

"Shit," he muttered as he saw Cassandra storming straight toward him.

"Logan! What the *hell* is this!? You ignore my calls, and I find you cheating on me with some slut?"

"Hey, bitch, I am *not* a slut!" Ashley wedged herself into the conversation.

"Oh, yeah? Then where the *fuck* are your clothes?"

Logan stepped out of the pool and rushed over to Cassandra, placing his hands on her shoulders. "Cass, Cass, it's not what you think. We were just messing around, that's all. I swear, I didn't cheat on you."

But she pushed him away. "If I didn't catch you, she'd be dick deep in you right now."

A perplexed look suddenly appeared on his face. "Why *are* you here, anyway? Were you spying on me or something? Trying to catch me in the act so you can hold it against me later on?"

The second those words came out of his mouth, he knew it was too late to reel them back in. "My cousin lives in Glendale, remember? Two fucking blocks away from this slut's house? God! I can't even look at you right now. You're clueless when it comes to my life, and I should never have believed you when you told me that bra I found in your car last month was your sister's. You don't even have a sister!"

Logan watched as she stormed off in tears, tearing off the necklace he had given her and throwing it into the sewers.

Shrugging it off, he went back to Ashley. "Where were we?" he asked, grabbing her waist again and pulling her close. She smiled at him, winking as she untied the knot holding the two halves of her bikini bottom together. He kissed her again, caressing her body as he'd caress the body of any sexy woman he was with, but the passion and intensity suddenly faded. He no longer felt anything toward Ashley, not even when she bent her head down toward his waist. It was all just…empty feelings.

"Wait, stop," he told her, lifting her head back up.

"Why? What's wrong?"

"I don't think I can do this anymore. Don't get me wrong, you're gorgeous, super sexy. I'm just not feeling it anymore."

She swam back to the deck and put her bikini back on, reaching behind her head to tie her hair up into a ponytail before crossing her arms over her chest. "It's because of that girl, isn't it?"

"What girl?"

"The mousy one. The bassist! The one who was *just* here!" She huffed. "You know, for someone so hot, you're kinda stupid. There's something clearly going on between you and that girl, and you should probably figure it out soon before you screw anyone else."

He didn't know what had overtaken him. He'd cheated on past girlfriends before, and he never felt any remorse, until now. Something about his relationship with Cassie just seemed to hit him at the core of his heart. He couldn't explain it, and he didn't want to admit it. Maybe, for the first time in his life, he actually felt love toward a girl.

Shaking his head, he tried to dispel the thought from his mind. *No, that can't be it*, he thought to himself. He looked over at Ashley again, trying to envision how her body would feel on top of his, but all he felt was disgust and shame.

Less than an hour later, he arrived home. Andrew was sitting on the couch, biting into a Big Mac, his feet propped on the coffee table, and his video game controller lying beside him.

"Hey, man," he almost choked on his pickle when he saw Logan walking in. "You're home early. I thought you're hanging out with Ashley."

"Got cut short," he murmured and grabbed a beer from the fridge. "Got any more of those?" he asked, pointing to the wrapper.

Andrew smiled sheepishly. "Sorry, just finished my last one. You said you weren't coming home until after dinner." He gestured his remnants over toward his direction. "Want the rest of this?"

"Nah, I'm good."

"Why *are* you home, anyway? Date didn't go so well?"

Logan shrugged. "You could say something like that."

But Andrew refused to let it go. He threw a skeptical look over in Logan's direction. "Something like that? Something's up with you. You're *never* home early on a Saturday. What happened?"

"I don't really feel like talking about it."

"Logan, I'm your *best friend*. I tell you everything about *my* life. Now, spill." Andrew polished off the rest of his Big Mac and took a large gulp of his coke.

"Fine." Logan groaned. He always hated talking about his feelings, even to those close to him. "It's Cass. She saw us."

Andrew blinked, his mind processing what he had just heard. "You mean, she—"

"Yup."

"Ooo, what'd she do?" Andrew winced, his empathic nature feeling Logan's pain.

"Nothing really, she just left. I think it might be over." He popped open his beer and took a sip. "The weirdest thing is, though, I've had this happen before. You were there. Never, not once, did I feel bad about any of it."

"So, why now?"

"I don't know. Maybe I'm—"

"In love with her?" Andrew interrupted.

"Maybe, I—wait, what am I even saying? No, I don't love her. I don't even think I'm capable of love. That's insane!"

"Could be, but I don't see what else would explain your guilt."

***

Cassandra's Story

"UGH! I *can't* believe him! I trusted him. I thought we were good together. I thought he actually liked me! You thought we were good together, right, Savannah?" Cassandra nudged her friend with her elbow as they sat on a bench at Papago Park.

Savannah was scooping a spoonful of blueberry water ice into her mouth when Cassandra almost knocked it out of her hand.

"Watch it!" Savannah exclaimed. "You can vent without feeding my food to the ducks."

"Sorry," Cassandra apologized. "But what am I gonna do? I can't forgive him, right? That would just give him the message that I'm fine with him cheating on me. I can't do that!"

Savannah scooped another spoonful into her mouth before putting it down beside her to avoid another potential accident. "Do you love him?"

"What do you mean?"

"Simple question, do you love him enough to push through and try to make it work? Or do you think he's just gonna cheat on you again?"

"I *do* love him. I just don't really…trust him," Cassandra admitted.

"Cass, it's not love if there's no trust. Think about it. What's the point of going back to him just to put yourself through something like that again? Wouldn't you rather just find someone who would never do that to you to begin with?"

"You mean, someone like Andrew?"

Savannah blushed. "Maybe. Andrew *is* really sweet, and I honestly don't think he'll ever cheat on me. Our love is strong, and we trust each other."

"Yeah, but you know, he *is* Logan's *best friend*. What if he rubs off on him?"

"Alright, now you're just trying to piss me off. Come on, we're going out tonight, and we're going to get you on top of another man to forget about Logan."

✳✳✳

Three hours later, Cassandra looked at herself in her hotel mirror from head to toe. She had on the tightest leather strapless dress she could find, well, Becca's leather dress, and heels high enough to break any man's self-esteem. She turned her brown locks into curls and polished her lips with the shiniest gloss.

"I don't need you, Logan," she said to herself in the mirror. "There are plenty of guys out there. I don't need you at all." She tossed her hair over her shoulder and headed out.

"How about that guy over there?" Savannah suggested as she pointed toward the stairs at the club.

Cassandra looked over and saw a rugged, well-built man with dark hair and a pointed nose.

"Um… I think he's taken."
"What makes you say that?"

She pointed over to the skinny redhead that had her arms wrapped around his, her body practically dangling off him as she leaned up to kiss him.

"Oh," Savannah said. "Never mind!"

"Ooo, wait, he's cute." Cassandra pointed toward the bar.

There was a man in his late twenties dressed in a black suit and silver tie. His hair was slicked back perfectly to match his slim physique, and there didn't seem to be any women within ten feet of him.

"Go for it," Savannah winked.

"Ugh, he's so sexy gorgeous. Be my wingman, please!" Cassandra begged, tugging on Savannah's arm until she finally gave in.

"Fine, but one of these days, you're gonna have to learn how to talk to guys without me."

Cassandra nodded, jumping up and down like a little girl who had just gotten her favorite Barbie doll for Christmas.

When they approached him, Cassandra could see the ringless finger on his left hand, and her face began to blush with excitement.

"Hey, what's up?" Savannah said to the man. "I'm Savannah, and this here is my friend, Cassie."

He finished off the rest of his whiskey and turned to face them. "Name's Dan. What are you girls drinking? On me."

"Just two beers, please." Savannah answered. "Actually, we came over to see if you're here alone tonight."

Dan winked at her after he ordered their beers. "Why? You interested in keeping me company?"

Savannah giggled. "No, not me. My friend here, Cassie."

Dan looked over behind Savannah to Cassandra, and then back to Savannah. He contemplated for a moment before saying, "Will you be joining us?"

"What?" Savannah asked.

"What?!" Cassandra repeated.

"Nothing personal, but you're so much hotter than your friend. It's either both of you, or…" He reached his hand over and slid it against Savannah's upper thigh, "Maybe you and I can just party by ourselves. I live in a penthouse." He winked.

But Savannah pushed his hand away and slapped him across the face. "Perv," she said. "And keep your damn beers. C'mon, Cass."

"Can you believe the nerve of that guy?" Savannah asked as they walked away.

Cassandra followed, her self-esteem shot. "Can you blame him? I mean, look at you! You're like Aphrodite, and I'm like your ugly friend. No guy will ever notice me if I'm standing next to you."

That's when Savannah stopped in her steps and whipped around. "Me?? You're the one who insisted that I be your wingman. If I'm 'impeding' you so much, go find your own guy."

Savannah's Story

Savannah stormed off in the opposite direction, leaving Cassandra all alone. She didn't even want to come out tonight. She was only trying to do something nice for a friend. And to think that's what she got in return. She walked toward the bathrooms and pulled her phone out of her purse.

Sorry we couldn't meet up tonight. Now I wish we had.

She sent the text to Andrew, only to receive a phone call seconds later.

"Hey," she answered.

"Hey, is everything okay? I was just about to call and check in on you when your text came through."

"Everything's fine, I guess. Tried to help Cass. I took her out tonight to try and make her feel better, but all I got in return was a cold shoulder. Now, she's off trying to hook up with whoever she can find, and I'm left behind by the stinky toilets."

Andrew laughed.

"It's not funny!"

"Sorry, I didn't mean to laugh. Want me to come pick you up? We can go grab some dinner."

"God, you have no idea how much I'd rather be doing that, but I can't just leave her here by herself. What if something happens to her, and I'm not there to help?"

"I get it. You're a great friend, and you don't always get the same respect in return. That's one of the things I love about you." Savannah could feel Andrew smiling on the other line as she smiled also.

"I'll see you tomorrow night?" she asked.

"I'll be waiting."

"I love you, Andrew."

"I love you too, Savannah."

When Savannah hung up, she looked around the club, but Cassandra was nowhere to be seen.

"Figures," she whispered to herself and found herself a high table by the window.

"Can I get you anything?" a waitress asked as Savannah sat down, adjusting her dress and propping her heels up.

"Cranberry vodka?"

"Sure thing."

The waitress walked away, and Savannah pulled out her phone again, scrolling through pictures of her and Andrew together, from the time his shoe fell off while they were hiking to the time he smeared whipped cream on her face and then licked it off. Savannah smiled.

Those were the days.

"What's a pretty girl like yourself doing all alone?"

She jumped, startled by the guy who rudely helped himself to the empty chair in front of her. He reminded her so much of Frank, deep eyes, long bangs, and a smile that could make any girl swoon. If Savannah was still single, he was exactly the type of guy she'd fall for back in the day. But things have changed now, and she was happy with Andrew.

"Can I help you?" she asked.

"No, not really. I was over by the booth with my friends and saw you here all alone. Thought I'd come over here and say hi. Hi! I'm Brad."

"Savannah."

"Savannah, such a pretty name! Can I buy you a drink?"

She shook her head. "Thanks, but I already ordered one." She leaned back so the waitress could place the glass on the table.

"Can I get you anything, sir?" the waitress looked over at Brad and asked.

Please don't order anything. Please don't order anything, Savannah thought.

She didn't ask for Brad's company, and she sure as hell didn't need him to have a reason to stay.

"Sure," he said. "I'll take a lager." Savannah rolled her eyes. This night was just getting worse and worse. She really didn't want to stay, but with Cassie still nowhere to be seen, she couldn't just leave. It was either stay put or wander around like an idiot.

"So, Savannah, why are you here alone? I'd never expect to find someone as beautiful as you in a club all by herself."

"I'm not. I'm with a friend. She's…somewhere."

"Ah, let me guess. She ditched you to go get laid?"

Savannah shrugged, then nodded. "Yeah, pretty much."

"I feel you. One of my friends did that to me less than an hour ago. Friends, always loyal until there's potential sex. Am I right?"

She laughed.

"You have such an affectionate smile," Brad said.

"Thanks."

As she took a sip of her drink, Brad studied her closely. "What are you looking at?" she asked.

"Oh, sorry, I didn't mean to be creepy, but you look oddly…familiar."

"I guess I just have a common face. I've been told that pretty often by people who confuse me with someone else." She took another sip and tucked a strand of her hair behind her ear.

"No, that's not it…" After a short pause, he suddenly said, "Wait, the Moonshines! You're the lead singer!"

"Guilty."

"Man, I knew you looked familiar! I've been to a few of your concerts, and I almost didn't recognize you at first without the makeup and iconic leather jacket. You guys are AWESOME!"

"Thanks, I can't take all the credit though. Wouldn't be where I am today without my band mates."

It took a while, but soon enough, Savannah began loosening up and finding comfort in talking to Brad. While Andrew supported her heart and soul, he was never really into her style of music, and Savannah never minded, but it was nice being able to talk to Brad about her thoughts and musings behind her tracks. He seemed to really understand her, understand where she was coming from with every lyric, every note, that she played.

It wasn't until several hours and several drinks later that Savannah found herself feeling slightly tipsy.

"Excuse me, I have to use the ladies' room," she told Brad as she stood up. But the vodka was hitting her harder than she had expected, and when she stood, she instantly tripped on her heel and fell over, with Brad right by her side to catch her.

"You good there? Need any help finding your way?" he asked when he caught her, holding her upper body in his arms.

"Thanks, I'm fine," she insisted, her hands grasping onto his biceps, his strong, muscular biceps.

And before she could even register what had happened, Brad leaned over to kiss her, their lips almost touching until Savannah blurted out, "I have a boyfriend," followed by a ball of vomit rising up her throat. "Excuse me."

She pushed him aside and bolted straight for the bathroom, throwing her head over a toilet bowl and unleashing the monster inside her.

Cassandra's Story

Cassandra found herself all alone as Savannah walked off. But she couldn't blame her. She deserved it. Savannah was only trying to cheer her up, make her forget about her cheating ex, but instead, she just drove her away.

"Why do I chase away everyone I love? What the hell is wrong with me?" she murmured to herself, not watching where she was going.

That's when she bumped into them. Logan and the slut from earlier, making out by the back doors, his hands sliding up her skirt.

"Are you kidding me?!" she screamed, loud enough for several party goers around her to hear. She marched over to them as Logan tried to speak, but her mind was so clouded that she didn't care what he had to say. She slapped them both, and then pointed at Logan, "We're done. For good. Fuck you, Logan."

"Cass, wait," Logan tried to speak.

"I said, FUCK YOU!"

She ran, as fast as she could and as far away as she could from them, refusing to stop until she was outside the club doors. Tears poured from her eyes, and she collapsed into herself by the side of the building.

How could I have been so stupid? And to think, I was going to forgive him and give him a second chance. I'm such a fucking idiot!

"This seat taken?"

Cassandra looked up and saw a cute guy staring down at her, pointing to the spot beside her. "You mean the ground?" she asked, confused.

He chuckled. "Yeah, I guess I do." Without waiting for an answer, he walked next to her and plopped himself down on the concrete, without a care that it was covered with gum and cigarette butts. "I'm Brad," he introduced himself, reaching out his hand for her to shake it.

"Cassandra."

"What's with the tears, Cassandra? Some guy break your heart?"

She stared at him blankly, surprised by his accuracy. "H…How'd you know?"

"I'm good. Psychic." He winked at her. "I'm just messing around. I saw you slap some dude before running out here. On behalf of all asshole men everywhere, I apologize."

That made Cassandra smile. "Thanks. I'm glad you're not all bad."

"I know *I'm* not," he winked again, leaning over to kiss her.

She could taste the lager on his tongue, and his lips engulfed hers as they maneuvered from her top lip to her bottom. She knew she shouldn't, but she was still so hurt over Logan that she didn't care who her rebound was. So, she kissed him back, allowing him to wrap one hand around her cheek as she placed her hands on his shoulders.

"Wanna go back to my place?" he whispered as he nibbled on her ear, his hands now sliding up her back and slowly pulling down the zipper.

"I can't," she whispered back.

As much as she wanted to, she couldn't abandon Savannah. She knew Savannah was still inside that club as she would never abandon her. Her one-night stand would just have to wait. She pulled a marker from her jacket pocket and wrote her number on his arm.

"Call me," she said, giving him one last kiss before heading back inside.

Chapter Seven: Andrew's Story

After his incredible and passionate night with Savannah, Andrew felt himself floating on the clouds. He never really imagined what his first time would feel like, but whatever it was, what he experienced was ten times better. Savannah was sexy, sensual, and she knew where and when to touch him to make him feel like he was on a turbo dose of LSD.

He couldn't stop smiling over the next several days, his happiness surging whenever he thought about his girlfriend.

Girlfriend, never in my life would I think I'd ever get the chance to say that.

He tried calling Savannah when he woke up, to see how her night out with Cassandra went, but his call went straight to voicemail.

She's probably still sleeping. I'll try again later.

He was expecting Savannah to come over later tonight, and he had to start getting ready. After the magical night they had together, he wanted all the nights they had together to be equally, if not more, magical.

First, he started by cleaning up his disgusting room. He *had* spent all of last night gaming, but he didn't think he made *that* much of a mess. Soda cans and crusty, stale pizza were thrown about, and a pile of dirty laundry sat by his closet, stinking up his room.

He still had much to do after cleaning up, including picking up some flowers for her and going to the grocery store to grab a few ingredients so he could make her favorite dish: chicken carbonara with prosciutto and green peas.

He was so excited to see her that he could barely get his mind to focus. Checking his phone again to see if she texted back, he saw nothing.

When he turned away, his phone sounded. He jumped onto his bed and grabbed it, expecting it to be Savannah.

Hey, Andrew! It's me, Vanessa. How are you?

Vanessa. He had almost forgotten about her. In fact, he never thought he'd actually hear from her again, as the meetup they had was bland and boring. He didn't have time to deal with her, whatever she wanted. He had to get ready for his night with Savannah. Deleting her text, he threw his phone back onto his bed and went into his closet to change.

Then his phone began to ring. His heart pumping again, he jumped onto his bed and answered it.

"Hello? Savannah?" he asked.

"Hey, Andrew! It's me, Vanessa!" the voice exclaimed excitedly on the other line.

God dammit…

"Hey…" he said.

"You didn't answer my text so I was worried that you might've given me the wrong number. Now that I know it's you, I'm so, so glad that it's the right one.

How've you been? I've missed you since our last conversation."

Andrew felt a little uneasy. He barely knew Vanessa, and now, she was telling him that she missed him. Part of him regretted not giving her a fake number after all. She *did* say she was flying home. It didn't cross his mind that he'd ever have to talk to her again. But on the other hand, it was this mentality that had lost him friends in the past, his antisocial personality thinking that everyone around him were psychopaths. Maybe it was time to change that, for himself, for Savannah. Maybe Savannah would like him to be more open with people.

"I'm good," he finally said after a long silence. "What's up?"

"Well, I have some good news…I'm back in Arizona! Actually, I guess I never really left. My family decided to make a detour and visit Utah before flying home. I stayed behind in Arizona while they went up north. There's just something about this state that makes me feel so…so…elated." She cleared her throat. "And I was thinking, that since we had such a good time hanging out last time, we could do it again. I'm free tonight!"

"Sorry, I can't tonight. I have plans."

"Oh, okay," her voice sounded disappointed but quickly recovered. "How about right now? Well, in about an hour. I'm free now!"

The discomforting feeling came back to his stomach. Last time he was out with Vanessa, he had gotten so caught up that he didn't make it back in time for Savannah. He couldn't have that happen again. But he also needed to go shopping to buy her some flowers. Maybe it couldn't hurt to have a woman's touch in picking them out. God knows he didn't know how to.

"Well, I do need to go out and buy some things. Wanna tag along?" he asked.

"I'd love to!" she shrieked over the phone, so loudly that he had to slightly pull it away from his ear.

He asked Vanessa to meet up with him at Beth's Florals in an hour, and when the hour struck, there she was. He waved at her and quickly checked his phone again. Still no message from Savannah.

"Hey!" she said, giving him a hug.

He hugged her back, but forced himself to pull away when her arms wrapped around him tighter.

"So, why are we here? Flowers for your mom?" she asked.

"No, my girlfriend, Savannah."

Vanessa's face fell. "Oh, I didn't know you have a girlfriend."

Andrew nodded. "I do. Shall we go inside?" He opened the door for her, and she hesitated for a moment, but proceeded to walk inside.

"Girlfriend, huh? You never mentioned a girlfriend."

"It's pretty recent. Happened right after we met. Besides, I didn't think I'd have to inform everyone."

She rolled her eyes, "Yeah, but it would've been nice to know. What are we looking for, anyway? Roses? Carnations? Daisies?"

"Yeah…I was kind of hoping you could help me out with that. I'm clueless when it comes to flowers." Andrew scratched his head as Vanessa wandered the store. Her navel was exposed from the cropped shirt she was wearing, and her jeans were so tight that he couldn't figure out how she fit her phone in the back pocket.

The silence between them was tense, and part of him suspected it was because he mentioned Savannah, but he didn't know why. Him and Vanessa were just friends. His relationship with Savannah had nothing to do with Vanessa.

Moments later, Vanessa reappeared in front of him, holding a bouquet of roses.

"These," she said. "She's gonna love 'em."

He looked at the price tag and frowned. "Eighty-three dollars? That's a little expensive."

"You wanna impress her, don't you? Trust me."

Against his better judgment, Andrew grabbed the bouquet and walked to the cash register. He was still hesitant. Savannah always said she hated it when Andrew bought her expensive gifts, but maybe Vanessa was right. Maybe Savannah was just being polite.

When they walked out of the store, Andrew checked his list. "Flowers, check," he said. "Now, I gotta stop by the grocery store."

"Do you mind if we stop by your apartment first?" Vanessa asked. "It's on the way, and I really gotta pee."

"I don't know…I *am* on a tight schedule. If I wanna get everything done before tonight, I don't really have time to make pit stops. Can't you just go at the store? They have a bathroom."

"No, I really can't. I have…have a fear of public bathrooms. The germs. The bacteria. Ugh! I can't. Please! I'll be quick. I promise."

Checking his watch, Andrew quickly did some calculations in his head. If they spent ten minutes max inside the apartment, he might still be able to get everything done in time if he ran to and from the store.

"Fine, but you better hurry."

Fifteen minutes later, they arrived back at the apartment. Logan had gone out, probably to another bar, and the place was silent and still.

"Bathroom's around the corner." He pointed toward the back.

As Vanessa ran for it, Andrew lied on the couch and pulled out his phone. Still nothing. At this point, he was starting to get worried. Savannah had never gone this long without texting him back. Something, or someone, must've happened at the club. He shook away his thoughts.

"No, she can't. She wouldn't. She would never cheat on me," he whispered to himself.

He dialed her number and called her again. Nothing. Nothing but another voicemail.

It took him awhile before he realized that Vanessa still hadn't come back. He got up and walked toward the bathroom, ready to knock to see if she was okay. Surprisingly, when he passed his room, he found her lying on his bed, her shoes kicked off, and her body spread out.

"Erm, what are you doing in here?" he asked.

"Andrew, your bed is SO fucking comfy. I love it!" she exclaimed, throwing her arms high up in the air and stretching out.

"C'mon, Vanessa, I'm serious. I'm already behind schedule. We have to get going." He tried to usher her out the door but found himself being pulled back.

"No, please, I wanna stay," she begged him, tugging at him to sit on the bed.

When he refused to move, she pulled herself closer, still holding onto his arm.

"Besides, I've been watching you all day. I know you've been checking your phone. What's the matter? Girlfriend didn't text back? Maybe she's out hooking up with some dude."

And just like that, his biggest fear realized. He couldn't be crazy if someone else confirmed it too, right? What if Savannah really was cheating on him. Could he just be wasting his time when she'd decided she never wanted to see him again?

"Andrew," Vanessa continued to speak. "Why don't, instead, you be with someone who *actually* cares about you? Someone you *actually* have something in common with?"

She reached her other arm out and pulled on his belt. When he didn't resist, she pulled even harder, until Andrew found himself on the bed with her.

Savannah's Story

"Fuck," Savannah moaned as she woke up.

She looked over at her alarm clock and saw that it was already late in the afternoon.

"Shit." Her head fell back against her pillow. "That's the last time I'm going out."

She never really had a problem with hangovers whenever she went out, but her fight with Cassandra made her want to drink all the stress away. She didn't realize how deep she had gotten herself into until she found herself puking her guts out in the club bathroom.

She wasn't even sure how she'd gotten home, what happened with Brad, or if she ever found Cassie. Her anger, mixed with the overwhelming sadness she felt from having to leave Andrew, made her feel so disconnected with herself.

Feeling the nausea come back, she ran to bathroom, puking whatever remnants of alcohol she had left in her stomach into the trashcan.

"Ugh," she moaned, reaching for the towel above her head to wipe herself off.

She dropped the towel beside her and leaned back against the tiled wall, pressing a hand against her forehead.

"Hey, Savannah!" She remembered Brad blocking her path as she tried to leave the club. "Why the rush?"

"I…I have to go," she answered, trying again to push past him.

But he only persisted more, grabbing her arms this time and pressing himself against her to keep her from moving.

"Let go! Let go of me!" She started to scream, but the club was so loud that no one, not even the bartenders or bouncers, could hear her.

Brad leaned in further, trying to kiss her, and Savannah struggled to pull away. She was already having a terrible night and didn't need some creep trying to have his way with her on top of all that. But he was too strong for her, gripping her with force and refusing to let go, until she heard Cassandra.

"Let go of her!" She screamed as she took off her heel and whacked him across the head.

Instantly, he let her go, his hands flying to soothe the bruise on his head. He whipped around. "What the hell was that for?"

Before he could say another word, Cassie screamed again. "You? You! You disgusting two-timing pig!"

Savannah didn't know what was happening, but she was also too out of it to care. She watched, her eyes squinting and head pounding, as Cassandra chased Brad out the door.

Her mind flashing back to her bathroom, she stayed put for a moment, trying to subside her raging headache, before reaching over for her phone. She'd wanted to call Andrew as soon as she got back to her hotel room last night, tell him that she loved him and that she was okay, but she must've passed out instead. She turned it on, and to her surprise, found six messages from him and ten missed phone calls.

She rushed to dial him back, but was sent to his voicemail instead.

"Come on, Andrew, pick up, pick up." With still no answer, she threw her phone against the carpet and hopped into the shower, hoping he'd call back by the time she was done.

Andrew's Story

"Vanessa, wait, stop." He tried to push her away as she reached up to kiss him. "I can't do this. I have a girlfriend. Savannah. I love Savannah."

She laughed, cackled. "Ha! Love? She can't even love you enough to call you back! Meanwhile, I drove all the way from the fucking Grand Canyon, TWICE, just to see you."

He pulled away from her grasps, backing into the corner of his room, and sunk to the floor. With his head down, he felt remorseful. "I know, and I'm sorry.

I thought we were just hanging out. I didn't mean to lead you on or anything. I'm sorry. But I love Savannah, and that's that."

"Dump her."

"What?"

"You heard me. Dump her, and date me. You know you'll be so much happier."

"What? No! And I really don't appreciate you saying things like that." He stood up and walked to the door. "I need you to get out, now. I don't think we can be friends anymore, Vanessa. Please go."

With a huff, she grabbed her shoes and stormed out, turning back as she reached the front door and said, "Don't say I didn't warn you. She's a BIT—"

"Bye, Vanessa." Andrew slammed the door behind her without letting her finish.

He looked down at his watch again and saw that over an hour had gone by. He was definitely behind schedule now, but he wasn't even sure if he wanted to continue with his plans anymore. Vanessa's words stuck like glue to his brain.

He still found himself contemplating when the bell rang again minutes later. Expecting it to be Vanessa, he swung it open and said, "I thought I told you—"

He stopped when he found Savannah at the door instead.

"Oh my god, Savannah, you're alive!" He wrapped his arms around her and hugged her. "Why didn't you answer any of my calls? I thought something had happened to you."

"Sorry, I was pretty hungover this morning," she said, hugging him back. "I tried calling you back, but you didn't pick up, so I decided to come surprise you instead. And who did you think I was?" She pulled back slightly.

"Huh?"

"Who'd you think I was when you opened the door? You don't usually get visitors, so who'd you think I was? Was someone else just here?" she probed.

"Oh, um, it was just Jehovah's witness. You know how annoying they can get." But his eyes refused to meet hers, and it didn't take long before she quickly noticed.

"Andrew…" she dragged. "Look at me."

With resistance and hesitation, he slowly turned his head, his eyes continuing to dart back and forth at a rate he couldn't control. His heart started beating faster and faster as she stepped closer toward him.

"You're hiding something," she probed. "I know that look."

"I'm not. I swear."

"Andrew…who was in your apartment?"

Sweat began spilling down his forehead and neck, and with daggers in Savannah's eyes, he couldn't hold it in any longer. "She's just a friend!" he finally blurted out.

With one brow raised, Savannah asked, "She?"

"Nothing happened, I swear! It's some girl I met online gaming years ago, way before I met you, and she messaged me the other day saying she wanted to meet up. I didn't think anything of it; I just thought it'd be cool to make some new friends, you know, since I don't go out much." He reached out and pulled Savannah into a hug.

"But then she started coming onto me when I was out buying flowers for you, and she told me to leave you, so I kicked her out. I'm so sorry, Savannah. I never meant to hurt you in any way. I thought her and I were just friends. I didn't know. Please, trust me, I didn't know."

His confession came out of him like word vomit, so quickly that he didn't even notice Savannah's struggle to keep up. Part of him knew he didn't do anything wrong, that his actions were all innocent, but a huge chunk of him felt overwhelmed with guilt and fear of losing the love of his life.

When Savannah didn't say anything, he grabbed her by the hands and led her to the couch.

"Please, Savannah, know that I would *never* do *anything* to hurt you. I love you with my entire being, and it pains me to know that I may have hurt you."

He reached over to the side of the couch, where his roses were still sitting. "Here are the flowers I got you. I meant to give you these later tonight. I guess that's ruined."

He tensed his shoulders, expecting to feel her wrath reign upon him, but instead, her face turned solemn. "Andrew, we need to talk."

"Please, don't be mad at me!"

She shook her head. "I'm not mad, but I have to fly home tomorrow. The tour's over, and I have to get back to my job, my life back in Portland."

He gripped her hands tighter. ""Ar…Are you breaking up with me?"

"That's what I came here to talk to you about. I love you, Andrew, I really do. But I'm not sure if we can continue this long distance. I have to be honest with you. Part of me almost cheated on you last night, while I was at the club, and based on what you just told me, it sounds like you almost did too. I think…I think we just live two very different lives. Me with my music, you with your gaming. And we live on opposite sides of the country. There are just too many factors against us, telling us no."

Andrew stared at her like a puppy who had just been kicked aside. "What are you trying to say?"

"I think you already know." Through her eyes, he could see a look of heartbreak, like she forced herself to say those words. He tried to hold back his tears as much as he could, but found a few coming out against his will. "I'm sorry," she sniffled. "Maybe one day, we'll cross paths again. Goodbye, Andrew."

She gave him a kiss on the cheek and left.

Chapter Eight: Andrew's Story

"Dude, cheer up," Logan said, throwing a popcorn kernel at him. "It's just a girl. You'll get over it. Look at me, I was all torn up about Cass, but I'm with Ashley now, and I've never been happier!"

"You don't understand," Andrew groaned. "She was my first love. She was perfect, everything I always wanted. I thought we'd end up together forever. And now, just like that, she's…she's gone." He grabbed a throw pillow and slapped it over his face. "I'll never love another woman again."

"Oh, stop being dramatic," his friend scoffed. "Everyone goes through the 'woe is me' stage after their first breakup."

"I'm NOT being dramatic!"

"Okay, okay, chill the fuck out, man. Just trying to help." He tossed back the rest of his soda and sat up. "How 'bout a bro night? We haven't done one of those in a while."

Andrew pushed aside the pillow slightly. "You're not gonna try and set me up, are you?"

"Nope! Just you and me. We haven't hung out since you started dating Sav...what's her face. I think it's time we get back into it. No girls, just us."

"I don't wanna." He maneuvered the pillow back over his face, but felt the force of another one bouncing off. "I just want to lie here all day and text Savannah."

"Don't you dare!" Logan smacked the phone out of his hands. "You send her even one text, and you're only showing her that you're too desperate and miserable to move on. And too bad. I'm tired of seeing you mope around. It's time you get off your ass and stop feeling sorry for yourself. We're going out tonight, even if I have to drag you."

Savannah's Story

"I still can't believe I broke up with him."

Savannah sat outside on her apartment balcony. Her feet were propped up on the railing, and she sipped an iced tea beside Becca.

"Why?" Becca asked. "No offense, Savannah, but he was kind of a loser. You deserve better, like Frank."

"Frank? Are you serious? He cheated on me so many times."

"So? He's an alpha. It's what they do. Doesn't mean you should just give up." Becca cleared her throat and took a sip of her drink. "I'm telling you, Savannah, letting Andrew go was the best decision of your life.

He didn't know anything about our music. He was holding you back."

Savannah shot her a look of fury. "He was supportive. Even if he didn't know much, he did the best he could. That's more than I can say about Frank." She stood up and walked back inside. "It's getting late. I think you should get going."

"Suit yourself," Becca shrugged. As she passed Savannah, she said, "But just remember, even if Andrew *was* the perfect guy, he's all the way in Arizona. You're not even in the same time zone. It would've never worked out."

"Bye, Becca." Savannah waved gingerly to her friend and closed the door behind her.

She looked around her apartment. Everything looked so foreign to her. She didn't spend that much time in Phoenix, but between her long nights in her hotel room and her time over at Andrew's, everything looked unfamiliar to her.

She walked into her bedroom and lied back on her pillows. She grabbed her teddy bear, Ruby, smiling at the time Andrew had spent hours and his entire wallet, determined to win it for her. When he finally did, he had spent more than triple what it would've cost to just buy it at the store. She admired his tenacity, his drive when he wanted something, refusing to let anything get in the way.

"Andrew," she whispered to herself. "Maybe Becca was right. Maybe you're not right for me, and we're just two kids caught up in the moment and foolishly fell in love."

She rolled onto her side and pulled out her phone. Still no messages from him. She was sure he'd text or call her by now. She missed seeing his name pop up on her screen every day, always wishing her a good morning or telling her he loved her. Scrolling back, she hadn't heard from him since the day she broke up with him. Sure, she had contemplated reaching out to him, but she knew that would only send him mixed messages. After her whole speech, she felt ashamed to pretend like nothing had ever happened. She couldn't hurt him like that, not again.

As she scrolled through the pictures of them together, smiling at how happy they both used to be together, a message from Frank popped up on her screen.

I miss you.

She hadn't seen or spoken to Frank since she called it off, so she was surprised to hear from him. She stared at the message, her fingers unmoving. She didn't want to answer. When she broke it off, she had no intention of turning back, and when she started dating Andrew, she thought she was done with Frank forever, that he had also moved on to whatever girl he'd picked up at a bar.

But now, here he was again, telling her he missed her. She didn't know how to react. She'd been with Frank for so long that, although a part of her will still always care about him, she didn't want to fall back in that trap, not again, not after the way he treated her all those years.

But she couldn't help but think back to what Becca had said, about her and Frank being perfect for each other. Frank *was* more in tune with her music and her band, and he also didn't live across the country. It just made more sense with Frank. She didn't love him; she wasn't sure if she ever really did, but the stars were just more aligned for them.

Andrew's Story

"Stop staring at your phone. She's not gonna call. Put it away and have some fun." Logan nudged Andrew on the arm. He handed him a beer and sat down across from him. "Tonight's about you. Look around. So many hot chicks here. Stop wasting your time focusing on just the one."

Andrew glared at him. He hadn't showered in days. Ever since Savannah left, he'd stop taking care of himself, spending all his days scrolling through the pictures of them on his phone. "She's not just another chick. I love her."

"How many times I gotta tell you? She's your first girl. You don't know if it's true love until you've been with several others." He pointed over toward the front door where a group of sorority girls were crowded. "I'm pretty sure at least three of them over there are horny. Go say hi. Maybe you'll get lucky."

"You know I can't do that."

"Why not?"

"I can't talk to girls, remember?" Andrew reminded him.

"Sure, you can. You got along fine with Savannah. Just do it again."

"I…can't. I don't know. It was just easier talking to Savannah. She was different."

Logan let out a loud groan. "Do I have to do everything for you? Come on, I'll be your wingman." He scooted out from the booth and grabbed Andrew by the wrist, dragging him toward the crowd.

"Hey, ladies," Logan said, winking at the girls in the crowd, who all giggled simultaneously. "I'd like you all to meet my friend, Andrew."

"Hey, Andrew!" They all shouted.

But instead of greeting back, Andrew felt a pit in his stomach, and his eyes were blinded by the luminescent lights above him. He could barely hear anyone's voice over the loud music, and his senses all went into overdrive that he found himself struggling to breathe. He tried waving back, but instead, bolted out through the double doors and heaved for air.

***

Things didn't get any easier after that. Logan attempted to take him out again, to socialize him with more people of the opposite sex to get his mind off Savannah, but he came up short time after time again. Andrew's nerves had been stabilized whenever he was around Savannah, his anxiety quelled, and his nervousness practically nonexistent. But with others, he started to remember why he never really dated in the first place.

"I give up, dude," Logan conceded after their sixth failed attempt. "I guess you'll just end up alone forever."

Andrew shook his head. "No, Savannah will come back. I just know it. We're meant to be together."

"Dude, Andrew, as your best friend, I need you to get this through your thick head. Savannah's gone! She's not coming back! She's probably shacking it up with some Portland jock while you're sitting here feeling sorry for yourself."

Andrew watched as Logan walked away. He understood where his frustration was coming from, and if Andrew could stop feeling down in the dumps, he would. He knew the logical thing would be just to move on, but Savannah.

He kept hoping that Savannah would eventually come back to him. With less than a 10% chance of that actually happening, he started to question what he was doing. Logan was right. Savanna *was* gone, and it wasn't like he could easily knock on her door and ask her to get back together. He didn't even know where she lived, just somewhere in Portland.

He pulled out his phone. Still nothing from Savannah. *Maybe she really doesn't care anymore. Maybe she really moved on."*

He pulled up his contacts, scrolled through the list, and dialed.

Savannah's Story

Savannah didn't know what she was thinking when she decided to text Frank back, asking him to meet up. The loneliness was probably catching up to her, and she missed the warmth of Andrew's arms around her. Whenever she thought of Frank, she wanted to rip her heart out and throw it in his face. Why she's considering giving him a second chance was beyond her.

She scrolled through more pictures of her and Andrew as she waited outside a café Sunday morning for Frank. Becca kept insisting that she get rid of them, get rid of everything that reminded her of her ex, but she couldn't.

Instead, she kept all her memories of him, including the texts they shared, in a secret folder, somewhere only she knew about. She could still feel him near her, kissing her neck and rubbing her shoulders. He was everything she'd wanted in a man. She even took his virginity, took his love, and was now letting it all rot away.

"Hey, Savannah." She heard Frank's voice.

When she looked up from her phone, she saw a whole different person. Frank was no longer the dirty hipster she'd known. He was actually cleaned up, with a brand-new haircut, a shaven face, and his clothes were crisp, featuring name brand tags.

"Hey, Frank," she said, putting her phone back in her pocket. "How've you been?"

"Pretty good, actually. I've stopped going out as much, and I'm even doing some online classes. Hoping to finally get that business degree I've been talking about for the past four years."

"That's great." Savannah forced a smile.

Frank certainly looked different, and it seemed like he was starting to make a change in his life, but whenever she looked at him, all she was reminded of was how bad he'd treated her, something she just couldn't get over.

"How's everything going with The Moonshines? When's your next tour?" He picked up one of the biscotti she had on the plate in front of her. "May I?"

She nodded. "Probably not until next year. Phoenix was our last big hurrah before the end of the year. Besides, we need new material before we can go back out there. But we'll see."

Frank bit into the biscotti, the crunch sending crumbs flying out of his mouth. "I'm sure you'll come up with something. You're the most creative person I know."

"Thanks."

"So, I'll cut to the chase. I'm sure you have better things to do than sit here and chit chat." He reached out and grabbed her hands. "I've missed you, Savannah, a lot. Ever since you broke up with me, I've been doing some self-reflection. I called it off with the other girl I was seeing. I'm sure you knew all about that anyway, and I haven't dated or hooked up with anyone since. For the past several months, I've been working on myself, bettering myself for you. Savannah," he said, moving closer to her and looking her in the eyes. "I want to give this another chance, give us another chance. We've been together for so long. We were good together."

"We were *not* good together," she reminded him. "You wouldn't stop cheating on me."

"Okay, fine," he admitted. "But we were good before that happened. Remember why we fell in love with each other in the first place?"

"Because of our love for music." She looked back up at Frank. He *did* seem different, gentler and more caring, but could someone like him really change, or was this all just a trap to lure her back in?

"Give me another chance, Savannah. We have so much history, it's insane to just throw it all away like that. And if you don't feel comfortable jumping all the way back in right away, let's take it slow. Whatever you want."

Savannah fell silent. Frank was right. They *did* have so much history, and he knew more about her than anyone else. All the signs were pointing for her and Frank to be together. Andrew was gone, probably with that Vanessa chick, and Frank, he was right here, ready to make it work again. Maybe it was just meant to be.

Andrew's Story

"Hello?" Vanessa answered.

"Hey, it's me."

"Andrew! I'm glad you called, though, I wasn't sure you'd ever call again after you so rudely kicked me out of your apartment."

Andrew scratched his head, then sighed. "Yeah, sorry about that. I was just having a bad day, I guess."

"So, how'd Savannah like those roses? She loved them, didn't she? I bet she did. Any girl would." She sounded eager and optimistic on the other line, like she was really enjoying their conversation.

"She did. I was actually calling to see if you wanted to go see a movie or something, if you're still in the area."

"I am, but aren't you, like, whipped or something? Won't Savannah murder you if she found out we went to the movies together?"

"No, we…we broke up, actually."

He hadn't said those words in a while, and it still stung when he did. It still felt so unreal. But then again, it also felt unreal that he even had Savannah in the first place. So, maybe their meeting wasn't fated. Maybe she was only meant to come into his life to push him into the dating scene, not with her, but with someone else, someone like Vanessa.

"Wow, did you actually listen to me and dump her?" Vanessa asked, the tone in her voice rising from the excitement.

"It doesn't matter. Do you wanna go to the movies or not?"

"I'd love to."

Chapter Nine: Andrew's Story

Three months had passed since Savannah went back to Portland and Andrew began dating Vanessa. Things had been good, but nowhere near as perfect and authentic as they had been with Savannah. Vanessa decided to stay in Phoenix while her family went back to New York. She assured Andrew that they were soulmates as they had so much in common, and she wanted to stay and see their relationship through.

However, several weeks into the relationship, Andrew felt ready to jump off the ship and swim away, or drown, whichever helped him get away from Vanessa sooner. At first, he thought Savannah was just like any other girl, that it didn't matter who he dated because he'd get along with them all the same. He didn't realize how wrong he was until several weeks in.

Other than her mild interest in Zelda, Vanessa wasn't much of a gamer at all, her hobbies focused more on shopping and Internet blogging. Her conversations were bland and one dimensional, and all she was ever interested in talking about was Andrew's past relationship, constantly comparing herself to Savannah and telling Andrew how much better off he was now.

"I don't think I can do it anymore," he told Logan one Friday afternoon after work. "I don't think I can be with Vanessa anymore. She's driving me insane."

"Why not just dump her then?" he suggested. "Just say bye and move on. Simple."

"I can't do that. I've never broken up with anyone before. What if she gets mad? What if she cries? I don't know how to let her down gently."

"So, what are you gonna do? Just keep dating someone you can't stand?"

"Maybe. It's not the worst thing in the world, right?"

Logan patted him on the back. "Take it from me, dude. You don't wanna do that. I tried that with Ashley. Wanted to drive a stake through my head after a month. It was so bad that I couldn't even tell her it was over. I just left. Blocked her. Ghosted her." He sighed. "Man, I miss Cass sometimes."

"What if I ride it out a bit longer? Maybe it'll get better. All relationships have their rough patches, right?"

But Logan only shook his head. "I don't know, dude. I've seen how you are around Vanessa, and I've seen how you were around Savannah. Big difference. Plus, Savannah's way hotter."

Andrew walked over to the kitchen, grabbed a bag of salt and vinegar chips from the cabinet, and picked up his phone.

Vanessa, he thought. *Of course.*

Ever since they started dating, she'd been texting him nonstop, asking how his day was every thirty minutes and sending pictures of herself to him.

Hey, Andrew. Whatcha up to?

He turned off his phone and sat at the kitchen table. He'd been ignoring her messages all day, too tired to deal with whatever she had to say next. Each conversation with her felt more stressful than the last, and it was all getting to be too much. In front of him, lied a picture frame, back facing up. He reached over and flipped it, only to find him and Savannah locking lips in front of Macchiaddiction.

He looked so happy, so in love. Vanessa hated coffee, so she never wanted to go there with him, preferring the new and trendy cafés in the downtown area instead, where she was more interested in taking pictures with her food than actually eating it.

"Savannah," he whispered to himself. "Why did you have to leave?"

"What do you feel like doing?" Savannah asked Frank one night.

He had come over to her apartment for dinner, bringing her a mess of Chinese takeout containers, and after eating in silence, Savannah needed something else to keep the night from turning into a dud.

She decided to give Frank another chance. Sure, he'd hurt her in the past, but everyone was capable of change, even someone like him. Their relationship had been good since they'd gotten back together. He refrained from staring at other girls and focused all his attention on her, much like how he did when they first started dating.

Frank shrugged. "How about a movie?"

"Sure, what are you thinking?"

Frank thought for a moment, and then spoke up. "How about Borat?"

"Borat? That's a terrible movie."

"It is," Frank admitted. "But Pamela Anderson's in it. She can make any shitty movie look good."

"No! We're not watching a crappy movie just because you want to see her jugs. We're picking something that's actually *good*." She picked the remote off the coffee table and started flicking through the streaming network.

"Alright, how about Blonde and Blonder? It's a chick movie. You like those, right?"

Savannah looked over at him, confused. "Why would you wanna watch a chick—Wait a sec, she's in that too! I thought you said you're over leering at boobs and butts!"

"I am," Frank replied, "but it definitely makes movies better."

Savannah spent the rest of the night scrolling through titles, unable to settle on anything with Frank. In the end, Frank decided to just leave as they were spending more time arguing than enjoying date night. When she closed the door behind him, Savannah sat back against her couch cushions.

She never had this much trouble with Andrew. Never an argument, and the only body he ever cared about was hers. She wrapped her arms around herself, pretending that Andrew's arms were wrapped around her. She snuggled against her pillows, closed her eyes, and reminisced on the time she and Andrew first made love.

But her thoughts were interrupted when her phone rang. It was Becca. She picked it up, and Becca started screaming on the other line.

"Savannah! You'll never guess! I just got a call from Clearfield Records. They want us to go back to

Phoenix to perform in the show they're hosting. This is it! Our big chance. What we've been waiting our entire lives for. We might actually get a record deal!!"

But Savannah couldn't hear anything other than Phoenix. She had mixed feelings about going back to the town Andrew lived in. What if she ran into him again? She knew she wouldn't be able to keep her emotions in check. She was with Frank now, but if she saw Andrew again, she feared she'd run back to him, and she'd have to break his heart all over again when she leaves.

On the other hand, he could've had another girlfriend by now and wanted nothing to do with her while she still had feelings for him. That would be even worse.

"That's…exciting, I guess. When do we have to fly out?"

"Day after tomorrow. I just need to convince Cass to go, too. She's going nuts about never wanting to be in the same state as that no-good-son-of-a-bitch jackass ever again. I'm guessing she means Logan."

"Logan, yeah." She paused in thought. Much like Cass, she didn't want to go back, not after everything that happened, but this was their big break, and she knew she couldn't be selfish just because she had problems with her love life. "Just send me the details. I'm in."

"Hey, Andrew, guess what we're doing this weekend. You'll either hate me or love me," Logan said as he came into his room one morning, throwing a shoe at him to wake him up.

"What the fuck, Logan?!" Andrew yelled, jumping up, startled.

"I have news!"

"What? That it's raining shoes?" Andrew asked, irritated.

He had spent all night tossing and turning, with constant nightmares about Vanessa following him and watching him. Every corner he'd turn, there she was, grinning at him with that buck-tooth smile of hers.

"Guess who's coming back to Phoenix?!" Logan exclaimed.

"The Pope? Wasn't he just here not that long ago?"

"Po—what? No, the Moonshines! Savannah's coming back to town! Aren't you excited? You've been nonstop bitching about how much you miss her for the past few weeks."

"No," Andrew simply said.

His stomach dropped. Sure, he missed Savannah, but he wasn't ready to see her, not after what happened. He couldn't see her. It'd just break his heart all over again, and he was finally starting to heal.

"What do you mean no? Isn't that what you wanted?"

"I can't. I'm not ready. Not like this. What if she sees me with Vanessa? What if she has a new boyfriend? It's too much. I can't."

"Andrew," Logan said. "Please, I need you there, for moral support. I've been trying to fake being okay, but I'm a mess without Cass. I need to tell her how I feel and apologize."

Andrew looked closer at Logan's face and studied it. He couldn't tell whether Logan was being serious or not, or whether he was just trying to mess with him. But when his frown didn't crack, Andrew reluctantly agreed.

***

Two days later, Andrew found himself at the concert, back in Logan's car, staring at the blinding neon lights. He didn't know what he would expect, whether Savannah would even care if he showed up. He kept telling himself that there wasn't a chance in hell they'd get back together. It was too far of a stretch, but still, he wore her favorite outfit, one that she always said brought out his beautiful eyes.

When they arrived, Logan went straight for the grass instead of wasting time finding an empty slot.

"Hurry up, I gotta go find Cass," Logan ushered him toward the stage.

But the déjà vu froze Andrew in his place. His anxiety of another rejection froze him in his place, and he struggled to move. "You go; I'll wait here. Sorry, I just can't. I'm not ready."

"Fine, but don't wander off too far. We may need to bolt if things get messy."

As Logan runs off, Andrew made his way toward the west side of the lot, straight for the tree stump where he and Savannah first got to know each other. He needed time alone to think, away from the noisy crowd. But when he approached closer, he saw a familiar figure already sitting on it.

"Savannah?" he called out.

The figure looked over at him, eyes wide with delight.

"Andrew!" Savannah exclaimed.

She ran over to embrace him, her arms locking around his neck, bringing back all the feelings he'd ever felt toward her. He hugged her back, wrapping his arms around her waist and pulling her in close. He knew he shouldn't, but feeling her body against his made him realize how much he still loved her.

"Andrew, there's something I need to tell you," Savannah said as they released each other. "I—"

"Still love you," Andrew blurted out.

"Am back together with Frank," Savannah finished.

His heart stopped. He felt like someone had just punched him in the stomach. He knew this would happen if he came to the concert. He knew she'd reject him, all his fears realized. He didn't want to confess, but seeing her made him remember how much he still wanted to be with her that he couldn't hold it in. His forehead began to sweat, his pulse racing. He didn't know what to say, how to handle the rejection from the woman he thought was his soulmate. Instead, he started to run. He didn't know where; he just needed to get away.

He kept running until he reached a creek nearby, sitting himself down by the rocks and watching the streams of water brush over the stones. His heart was still racing, and his breath still short, but the calmness of the waters and the distance from Savannah started to bring sanity back into his life.

He tossed a rock into the water, watching it skip as circles formed from where it made its impact.

Snap!

He turned around at the noise and saw Savannah, who walked toward him and sat down beside him. He wanted to run again, but he didn't know where else he'd go. And it didn't matter. She'd only follow him again.

She remained quiet for a moment after she sat down, staring out into the water and throwing a few rocks over the waves.

"I'm sorry, Andrew, for everything. I know how much I've hurt you."

He didn't answer. He didn't know what else to say. Every word that wanted to come out of his mouth was a confession of his feelings, and after that painful confession from Savannah, he figured the best way to keep himself from getting hurt was to just shut up.

"I never stopped thinking about you," she continued.

That caught his attention. "Really?" he asked, turning his head in her direction.

"Yeah," she answered. "Truth is, I still have feelings for you. I still love you. I just know I can't, because of the distance, you know?"

"Is that why you got back together with Frank? Or did you never stop loving him either?" He tried to keep his tone from sounding angry and bitter, but the jealousy that raged inside him was far more powerful. "Andrew, please, I don't love him. I love *you*." She looked over at him, staring into his eyes and running a hand through his hair. "Honestly, I don't know why I got back together with him. I think it was a combination of loneliness, Becca saying how perfect Frank is for me, and his promise to change, which, of course, he didn't. But I never stopped loving you, missing you."

She leaned in closer to him, their foreheads pressing together. "I still love you, Andrew."

She kissed him, her lips warm and soothing like Andrew had remembered them to be. He felt his heart shiver, the sparks flying from his first kiss with

Savannah. He grabbed her face with his hands and pulled her in closer, wrapping his tongue around hers and kissing her with a fiery passion. He leaned her back onto the grass, their bodies still pressed against each other, as he continued to taste her lips.

"I love you," she said again when she had a moment to breathe, but instead of saying it back, he continued to kiss her, from her lips to her neck, reaching a hand up her shirt.

"I can't," he suddenly said, stopping and stepping away from her.

"What's wrong?"

"I can't do this. I can't get hurt by you, not again. You're with Frank. I don't fucking know why, but you're with Frank, and you'll always go back to him. You're just going to leave again, and I can't get sucked back in. I'm with Vanessa. You're with Frank. That's just how it's supposed to be." He stood up and started to run away.

"Andrew, wait! Don't go!"

"Just…Just stay away from me! Forever!" he shouted back, leaving her by the creek all alone.

Cassandra's Story

"Cassie!" Cassandra heard her name from far behind her and turned around, seeing none other than Logan Matthews running straight in her direction. He wore a white blazer and dark blue jeans, his hair slicked back, and his face cleaner than she had ever seen it before. He held a bouquet of carnations, her favorite flowers, in one hand and waved to her with the other.

"Oh, great," she muttered to herself. She tugged at Becca's arm. "Hey, Becca, don't you think we should be getting ready? Where's Savannah? Maybe she's backstage already. We should head up there."

But Becca only turned around and looked at her like she was crazy. "We still have over an hour. Just relax. Grab a beer or something. Might loosen you up."

Frantic to get away, Cassandra looked behind her again and saw Logan fast approaching her. She picked up her bass and started to walk away, but felt a grasp on her arm instead.

"Hey, Cass," Logan said, panting out of breath when he finally caught up to her.

Cassandra could only sigh with annoyance. She still hated Logan for what he'd done to her, and she wanted nothing more than to never see him again. "What?"

"C…Can we talk?" he asked, looking over at Becca. "In private?"

"Why? So, you can tell me how many times you got laid?" She started to walk away again, but Logan was much stronger than her.

"Please, Cass, just give me five minutes. It's all I ask." He held out the flowers. "And these are for you. I know how much you like them."

"Fine," she said, grabbing the carnations. "Five minutes."

He led her over to an empty bench behind the stage and sat her down. He then sat down beside her and tried to hold her hands, but she pulled them away.

"Sorry," he apologized with his head down.

"What did you want to tell me?"

"God, I don't even know if you'll believe me, but I want to apologize, for everything. For hurting you, for cheating on you, everything."

"For putting your dick in some other girl?"

"That, too. Look, I know I haven't exactly been the best boyfriend. I've done many terrible things in my life that I wouldn't even know where to begin fixing them even if I wanted to." He looked up at her. "But out of all those things, hurting you was the one I regret the most. To be honest, when we first started dating, I saw you as just another girl to hook up with, nothing more. But when you caught me that day with Ash— her, I knew I'd fucked up. I just felt so guilty afterward, like I had done something I shouldn't, and then it clicked."

He grabbed her hands again, this time, she didn't pull away. "Cass, I'm in love with you. I've been with many, many girls before in my lifetime, but I've never really felt…love. I don't know why. I can't explain it, but ever since you left, I've been a mess. I tried replacing you. I've had sex with more girls than I even want to admit, but the entire time, all I could think about was you."

"Is that supposed to impress me? You telling me how many girls you fucked?"

He shook his head. "No, and I'm not saying any of this so you'll forgive me or give me a second chance or feel sorry for me. I don't expect anything from you." He stood up, his fingers sliding off hers. "I guess my five minutes is up. I just needed you to know how I felt. I'll see you around, Cass."

Cassandra watched as Logan walked away. She remained seated, more confused than ever. She couldn't tell whether Logan meant everything he said or whether he was only playing her for a fool. She thought she'd moved on. That kiss with Brad was supposed to bring her a new love, but it only made her feel ashamed and sick to her stomach. She didn't want to admit it, but she still wanted Logan in her life. As much as she tried to hate him, he never really left her heart.

Fighting the internal battle with herself, she gritted her teeth, clenched her fists, and got up, running after him while tripping over herself. "Logan!"

As soon as he turned around, she leaped into his arms and kissed him hard, wrapping her arms around his neck and refusing to let go. Five minutes later, she released her lips and pressed her forehead against his, smiling.

"I must be crazy, but I'm in love with you, too."

He grinned, held her even tighter, and kissed her again.

Becca's phone rang as she began unloading her drum set. It was Frank.

"I told you not to call until I got home," she hissed into her phone, walking into a solitary corner backstage, away from people.

"Sorry, babe," Frank said on the other line. "I just miss you too much and wanted to hear your voice."

Becca felt her heart warm and placed a hand over it. "Aw, you're so sweet."

"So," Frank continued. "When do I get to feel your naked body again? You know how much I love that moist pu—"

"Shhh! We don't speak about that, remember? Only in person! Savannah doesn't know, does she?"

"Why would she? If she hasn't figured it out in the past two years, there's no way she would now."

"Good." Becca smiled. "And it's gonna stay that way. I'll be home in a few days. In the meantime, send me some pics. I'm feeling a little…unsatisfied."

Becca hung up and sat down with her drums. She knew what she was doing was wrong, how much she was betraying Savannah and her trust by sleeping with Frank. But after all, she *did* steal him from her.

She remembered the days, when they were still in college. Becca had always loved Frank, ever since she saw him lifting weights at the gym, his well-defined muscles ripping through the muscle tee he had on. And Savannah knew that. She even offered to talk to him for her, see if he liked Becca back.

But when they approached him, Frank only had eyes for Savannah, staring at her like she was a prized trophy while Becca was nothing but the ugly sidekick. It didn't take long before they started dating. And people expected them to. They were like Beauty and Prince Charming. Savannah had always been better looking than Becca, something she could never get past, and so, she got all the guys Becca wanted.

Most of the time, it didn't matter. It had always been that way. But with Frank, she couldn't let it go, and she had always hated Savannah for it. Savannah knew she liked Frank, but she agreed to go out with him anyway, eventually moving in with him.

But it didn't matter in the end. Two years ago, while Savannah was off at work, Becca went to visit Frank. One thing led to another, and they hooked up, and they hadn't stopped since, hiding it from Savannah to prevent their band from falling apart.

She sighed, coming back to the present and watching the lights glow brighter as they approached further into the night. She could've had Frank to herself. Savannah had come so close to breaking up with him so many times that it would've been easy for her to be with him, especially so when Savannah was with Andrew.

But the thrill, the excitement. She loved the secrecy, sneaking around behind her back, fucking her boyfriend, almost like she was getting back at her after all these years of sisterhood betrayal. She didn't convince her to get back together with Frank for

Savannah's sake; she did it for her. Frank was hot, don't get her wrong, but he could never be a good boyfriend; she could never love him. But revenge, that was something she did love. And she had no intention of stopping.

Chapter Ten: Andrew's Story

Andrew Cohen woke up the morning after the concert. His head was throbbing again, and he felt like he was on the verge of passing out. He couldn't even fully remember what had happened the night before. One minute, he was kissing Savannah, and the next, he was drinking his weight in beer at a bar.

"Savannah," Andrew whispered. "What happened?"

He reached over and picked up his phone. No messages. He couldn't recall whether last night really happened.

Savannah is in Maine, isn't she?

Scrolling through his short list of contacts, he found her name and dialed. No answer.

He dialed again.

Still nothing. Nothing but her voicemail.

Throwing his phone aside, he pulled on a t-shirt and went downstairs, where he was surprised to find Logan having breakfast with Cassandra.

"Cassandra?" Andrew asked. "What are you doing here? Aren't you supposed to be in Maine?"

But she only gave him a skeptical look. "No… We had a concert here last night, remember? Savannah wanted to fly back today, but I convinced her to stay a few extra days so I could spend time with my little peanut butter cup." She smiled and leaned toward Logan, snuggling their noses together before giving each other a kiss.

"Barf… Wait, Savannah? She's here? In Phoenix?" he asked, suddenly realizing what she had just said.

"Um…yeah? Don't you remember? You pretty much told her to fuck off last night," Cassandra reminded him.

"What? No, I didn't. I would never. I love her. I tried calling her earlier, but I kept getting her voicemail."

She shrugged. "Well, from what I heard, you told her to stay away from you, forever. I'm gonna take a wild guess and say she blocked your ass."

"What? No. Why would I say that? That couldn't have been me. Tell her to unblock me!" Andrew screamed. "Tell her!"

"Dude, Andrew, chill the fuck out. Cassie didn't do shit. Maybe instead of yelling at her, go make this right." Logan stepped in. "Something clearly happened between you two, and if you wanna fix it, you should go find her before it's too late."

"Fuck!" Andrew turned to Cassandra. "Where are you guys staying?"

"Why? So, you can make her cry even more?"

Andrew was taken aback, a pained expression crossing his face. "I…I made her cry?"

"All night."

Andrew fell to his knees in front of Cassandra. "Please, please tell me where she is."

"Come on, Cass. The poor man's hopelessly in love. Throw him a bone," Logan added.

She took a deep breath and said, "Fine, Luxor Hotel. Don't make me regret this."

"Thank you! Thank you!" Andrew gave her a hug, grabbed his phone from his room, and within ten seconds, he was out the door.

"Can I get a small latte, please?" She pulled out her credit card and swiped it on the reader at Macchiaddiction.

"You're Andrew's friend," Ms. Madge said as she handed her the cup. "I remember seeing you two here together."

"Huh? Oh, yeah." She grabbed the cup and impatiently waited for her receipt. She didn't want to be associated with Andrew. She just wanted to get out of this town and never come back.

"Is he doing any better? He comes in here every Saturday, but lately, it just seems like something's bothering him."

"Oh, um, I'm sure he's fine. I have to go. Thanks for the latte."

She quickly snatched the receipt out of the woman's hand and left, eager to get as far away from memories of Andrew as possible.

But when she walked back out, all she saw were things that reminded her of him, of the times they spent together, of their dates. She looked over at the hot dog stand and remembered the time he squirted mustard all over his shirt because the cap was clogged. She looked over at the tattoo parlor, remembering the time they almost got matching tattoos before their fear of needles scared them out of it. Everywhere she turned, all she could see was him.

She sighed, sadness in her eyes. She took a sip of her drink and headed to the creek, the place she and Andrew last spoke. She sat down by the rocks and drank her latte, watching the fish swim about and the frogs leap from lily pad to lily pad.

She closed her eyes, thinking back to the day she first met him. He was so shy and different, yet so compassionate and gentle. He remembered falling for him instantly, from the first time their hands touched to the first time they kissed. Everything just felt so right, so perfect.

But that was all over now. He didn't want anything to do with her anymore, shutting her out of his life forever. And she understood why. She had loved him in so many ways, but she was also the biggest reason he was so afraid of being with her. She deserved it. Andrew had been nothing but a gentleman, the perfect boyfriend, and she left him to go back to Frank, of all people.

Maybe her mother had been right all along. Maybe she *did* have a problem with commitment, driving away those who were good for her and falling for all the wrong people.

Andrew's

Story

Andrew raced inside Luxor Hotel and ran up the stairs. The girls' room was on the fifth floor, but his heart was racing so fast that he didn't have time to wait for the elevator.

"506, 506," he whispered to himself, looking from door to door. "506!"

He knocked on the door, reciting his speech in his head while he waited for Savannah to answer. But the door remained closed. He knocked again, this time, he heard giggling from the other side.

"Savannah! Savannah! I know you're in there. Please, open up. I need to talk to you."

But still, no one answered.

He knocked even harder, continuing to scream her name, until finally, the door swung open with Becca standing at the door, holding a robe up to cover herself.

"Ugh, Becca, where are your clothes?" Andrew asked as he shielded his eyes.

"Hey! It's *my* room! You don't see me knocking on *your* door and asking you where *your* clothes are. What the hell do you want?" she demanded.

"Savannah. Is she in there? I really need to talk to her." He tried to look inside, catching his eyes on a pair of male shoes, before Becca stepped in and blocked the rest of his view.

"She's not here."

"Where is she?" he probed.

"How the *fuck* should I know? She's not here. Now, leave, please."

"Please, Becca, just tell me where she is!"
"I said, I don't know!" She slammed the door in his face before even waiting for his response.

Distraught, Andrew tried calling Savannah again, with no luck. He didn't know what to do next. He had messed up, big time, and it may have been too late to fix it. As he walked down the steps of the hotel, his phone rang.

Flustered, he fumbled through his pockets and pulled it out. Vanessa. He hadn't spoken to her in weeks, constantly screening her calls and deleting her messages. He still didn't know why he even dated her. He found her excruciatingly annoying and nothing like Savannah.

But as soon as he put his phone away, he heard a scream from behind him. He turned around and saw Vanessa running in his direction.

"Andrew!" she yelled. "Why haven't you been picking up my calls? I've texted you. I've called you. And nothing. That's *not* how you treat your girlfriend. I demand an apology. Now!"

"Vanessa… I can't do this," he began.

"Can't do what? Apologize? Of course, you can. Just say sorry, and we can go grab some ice cream. There's this new place that just opened up called H2O, and I'm DYING to check it out."

"No, Vanessa. I can't do this anymore. I can't be with you. I don't love you. I never have."

Andrew couldn't believe how easily the words rolled off his tongue. He had taken so long to break up with Vanessa because he didn't know whether he could handle hurting someone. But his desperation to only be with Savanah must have driven him to do the unimaginable, to leave the woman he never loved.

But Vanessa didn't shed a tear. She didn't get mad. She just…laughed. "Very funny, Andrew. Stop messing around. Alright, no apologies necessary. Let's go, I'm starving."

Andrew refused to budge, stuck in his place as Vanessa tried to drag him.

"Wait, are you serious? Are you really not gonna come?"

"I'm serious, Vanessa. We're done."

"It's that bitch, isn't it? Savannah? You're still in love with her!" Her voice was growing louder, and Andrew felt her attaching to him more.

"I'm sorry, Vanessa, but I have to go."

Tears flowing from her eyes, Vanessa held onto Andrew's arm and asked, "Can I at least have one last hug? As a last farewell?"

Andrew shrugged. He didn't see any harm in one last hug. After all, he owed her at least that for acting like a jerk around her. He knew what he was doing to Vanesa wasn't fair, that he was so focused on Savannah he didn't care who he hurt along the way.

So, he nodded, reaching out his arms to pull her in, feeling nothing but coldness and indifference around her. As he tried to pull away, he felt her lips against his, her hands grasping his head so tightly that he struggled to pull away.

"Vanessa, stop! It's over!"

But when he turned around to leave, he saw Savannah staring right at them.

Her sadness broke his heart, and he chased after her when she started to run. He couldn't believe what he had just done. All this time, searching for her, and he only managed to hurt her even more.

He finally caught up to her when she slowed down at the bridge, her body sinking down to the concrete ground as she cried into her hands.

"Go away!" she shouted as Andrew approached her.

"Savannah, please, let me explain." He knelt down next to her, and she cried into his arms, only to push him away seconds later.

When she finally did speak again, her words were not what Andrew wanted to hear. "We're not good for each other, Andrew. We never were. Just two crazy kids who fell in love. Maybe I was just grieving over my parents, or maybe I just wanted a reason out of my relationship with Frank that I fell in love with you without actually loving you. But I need to stop lying to myself. We're not soulmates. We're nothing. There's just too many obstacles that always come between us."

She stood up and walked out further to look down into the water, with Andrew standing up shortly after and following her. He walked behind her and placed a hand on her shoulder.

"Don't," she said and shrugged it away.

"I love you, Savannah."

"No, you don't. You just think you do because I was your first, but there are so many other opportunities and dating experiences for you that you don't know about yet. Once you get back out there, you'll see that we were never meant to be."

"You're wrong." This time, he walked behind her and wrapped his arms around her waist, resting his chin on her shoulder. "I know what love is, and I know it's with you. I'm sorry for the way I acted last night. I was just hurt, first by you leaving, and then by you getting back together with Frank. It was all too much to handle." He snuggled his face into her neck. "But none of that matters to me anymore. I love you, and I don't care about any of it except being with you."

Savannah took a deep breath, her body melting into Andrew's arms before pulling away again and walking further in.

"I can't, Andrew. We don't belong together. We live in different worlds. I love Frank, and you love Vanessa. That's just how it's supposed to be."

"Savannah, please, don't do this. Don't act like you don't feel the same way I feel." He followed her, grabbing her waist again and spinning her around, leaning his face in closer to hers and breathing heavily. "I know you feel the sparks when we're together. It's a feeling I've never felt before, not even with Vanessa, and I don't want to let that go." He lifted a hand and gently caressed her chin.

"Andrew, no…"

"It's okay. We're meant to be together. I just know it." He leaned down to kiss her, shivers shooting down his spine when she kissed him back. "I just want to do that all the time."

"Me too," Savannah agreed.

But when Andrew leaned back down to kiss her again, she stopped him. "I love Frank."

"You're kidding me, right? That guy has done nothing but hurt you."

"It just makes sense to be with him," she shook her head and said. "I belong with him." She pulled away from Andrew's grasp and walked away.

Chapter Eleven:

Savannah's

Story

A week later, back in Portland, Savannah was determined to make her relationship with Frank work, for good. She threw on her sexiest outfit, with as much cleavage as she could show, and decided to bake a pie to surprise her boyfriend with. She wanted it to be romantic, show up at his front door, kiss him, and spend the night together, just the two of them.

Andrew had called her twice since she got home, but she couldn't bring herself to answer it. She contemplated just blocking him altogether, but she couldn't bring herself to do that either. She loved seeing his messages and calls come through. Even though she knew she couldn't answer them, they still made her feel like he cared.

When she arrived at Frank's front door, she smoothed out her dress and knocked, tossing her hair back over her shoulder and adjusting the strap of her bag. She heard fumbling on the other side before Frank finally opened the door, shirtless and wearing nothing but a pair of boxers.

Savannah raised a brow. She knew Frank, all too well, and him in boxers usually meant he was up to something.

"Savannah! Hi! I wasn't expecting you. What brings you by?" he asked.

"Nothing really, I just wanted to surprise you with this pie. I thought we could spend the day together, just you and me."

"Yeah…now's not exactly the best time." He faked a cough. "I feel like I'm coming down with something."

She didn't believe him for a second. "Who's in there?" she asked.

"What? Nobody. What are you talking about?"

"Oh, come on, Frank. You've been cheating on me for years. You really think I'm that stupid?" She pushed hard on his door, sending it flying open, preparing herself to see whatever bimbo he picked up from the club this time.

To her horror, she found Becca, naked and under his sheets, sitting on his couch. The worst part was, she didn't look embarrassed or ashamed. She didn't have a look of guilt or remorse. She just smirked.

"Becca?! You? How could you!?"

"What'd you expect, Savannah? Admit it, you never liked Frank, anyway. You just saw him as security. He deserves better than you." She pulled out a cigarette and lit it, puffing the air and blowing it at Savannah.

Savannah turned back to Frank. "Why? After everything you told me when we got back together. Why? Is this because I said I was too tired to come over on Tuesday?"

Becca laughed, her voice so loud it sounded like a cackle. "Are you *really* that stupid, Savannah? We've been fucking for the past two years. I'm surprised it actually took you this long to figure it out."

"Tw…tw…two years?!"

She turned back to Frank, then back to Becca, both of whom looked completely apathetic, neither one saying a single word to her.

She felt her heart cracking, her lungs constricting, and she knew she had to get out of there. She dropped the pie, stepping on it as she turned around and ran down the hall. She continued running, even after she left the building, her legs moving faster and faster, unable to slow down until she found herself at the pier.

She fell to her knees by the dock, catching her breath and gasping for air. Everything had been so perfect, so in place, and now, she felt like her entire world was falling apart.

She pulled out her phone, about to call Cassandra, but realized that she may not be on her side. In fact, she may have also known about Becca and Frank. She didn't know who to trust. She didn't have anyone to turn to, other than…

"Hey," Andrew said as he picked up the phone.

"Hey," Savannah replied. She tried to catch her cool, but she couldn't hide the fact that she'd just been crying.

"I'm so glad you called." When Savannah didn't say anything, her words replaced by sniffles instead, Andrew asked, "Hey, Savannah, is everything okay?"

"No," she whispered.

"What's wrong? Savannah, it's me. You can tell me anything, remember? I'll always be here for you, no matter what."

"I fucked up, big time. I gave up the love of my life for someone I don't even like, all just to have it explode in my face. I'm such an idiot."

"You're not an idiot," he reassured her. "You broke up with Frank?"

She shook her head, "No, you. I never should've left."

"I wish you didn't."

"I messed up, didn't I? I messed up any chances I could've had with you."

Andrew paused, then spoke up. "No, you didn't."

"What?"

"Turn around."

When Savannah turned around, she found Andrew standing behind her, dressed in a suit and holding a single rose.

"What? How'd you—"

"Cass. She told me where I might be able to find you," he said. He closed in on her. "I couldn't stop thinking about you, since you left. I didn't want to just give you up so easily. I knew it wasn't over. That's why I flew up here, to convince you that we're meant to be." He got down on one knee, pulling a small box from his blazer pocket. "This is my last-ditch effort. I have nothing left to lose. Savannah Cassidy, will you marry me?" He opened the box, and inside, a diamond ring sat perfectly in place.

Savannah was speechless. She had gone through so many emotions in one day that she no longer knew which one was appropriate except to freeze. She looked at Andrew, his face still as handsome as the day she first saw him, and his love for her still as strong as the day they first made love. Still struggling to get her words out, she nodded, tears pouring from her eyes, and a smile forming on her face.

Andrew grinned, a smile so wide that Savannah knew she made the right choice. Andrew had always loved her, through thick and thin. He really *was* the perfect man for her. He ran over to her, placed the ring on her finger, and picked her up, spinning her around in the air before leaning down to kiss her.

"I'm truly the luckiest man alive," he said, kissing her again.

She locked herself around him, promising herself that she'd never let go ever again. Andrew was her world, her soulmate.

✻✻✻

Andrew's Story

A month later, the day before their wedding, Andrew surprised Savannah with a limo outside their apartment. They had been living together in Portland ever since they got engaged. The Moonshines had broken up, and Cassandra moved to Phoenix to live with Logan. As for Becca and Frank, no one had ever heard from them again, with rumors from their distant friends saying that they had eloped and moved to London.

"A limo?" Savannah asked as she walked outside, still in her pajamas.

"How about we skip the wedding and run off together instead?" he asked.

Without hesitation, she squealed and ran toward him.

"Savannah, watch out!" Andrew screamed, reaching his arm out toward her.

But when Savannah turned around, it was too late. The truck collided into their car, sending Savannah soaring through the air before landing on the opposite side of the street.

"Savannah!" Andrew cried out in agony. "Someone call 911! Someone, please, call 911!"

He rushed over to Savannah's side, pulling off his jacket as he ran. Her body was lifeless when he saw her up close. Her face had been scuffed, and trails of blood were trickling down her face. Andrew fell to his knees, slowly lifting up her head and placing his jacket beneath it before resting her head back down.

"No, no, no, Savannah, please stay with me. The ambulance will be here soon. I'm here. I'm here. I promise I won't leave your side. I promise."

He leaned down and pressed his head against hers, praying to God that she was going to be okay.

***

"I'm sorry, Mr. Cohen," Savannah's doctor, Dr. Metz, said several months later. "Savannah's showing no signs of progress, and truth be told, I'm not sure how long she's going to be in this coma. Even if she does wake up, due to the length of time, there's no guarantee that she's going to survive much longer. There was severe damage to her brain. Our best advice is that you pull the plug."

But Andrew shook his head. "No, no, it can't end like this. I know she'll wake up." He turned to Savannah, "Please, Savannah, please pull through. I love you. You're my wife, my soulmate, my everything. I don't want to be in this world without you."

He kissed Savannah on the hand, and then her lips, before resting his head on her chest.

"I'll give you some time to make your decision," Metz said as she left the room, leaving Andrew behind in tears.

❉ ❉ ❉

Andrew Cohen never left Savannah's side. When her insurance no longer covered her medical bills, the hospital had no choice but to send Savannah home with Andrew. He was lost. He didn't know what to do, still unsure of whether Savannah would ever awaken. Sighing as he opened his car door, he carried Savannah into their home, placing her on their bed.

Day in and day out for the next several weeks, Andrew cared for Savannah, cleaning her and never leaving her side. He continued to hold onto the hope that, one day, she would find the strength to fight through the fear holding her back. Savannah was his first love, and Andrew never forgot that.

"Hey, Andrew, long time no see. You still with that singer from that band?" Vanessa asked one day while Andrew ran out to grab a cup of coffee and a couple muffins in case Savannah woke up.

"Hey…Vanessa…Savannah? Yeah, we're engaged, actually."

She chuckled. "Last time I heard, she was a vegetable. Don't you think it's time to move on to someone else, you know, someone who doesn't just sleep all the time?"

Andrew rolled his eyes. Typical Vanessa. "What, you mean someone like you?"

"Well, I *have* been doing pretty well for myself. I've been eating healthier, just got a new job, bought the swankiest apartment. I could take care of you, you know? I'm sure, now that you no longer have that luxury and fame, you must be struggling, taking care of yourself *and* another person." Vanesa flipped her hair back, "I could take care of you, give you everything you've always wanted. What do you say?" She slid her fingers up and down his biceps. "Hmm, still as manly as I remembered."

Andrew pulled back from her touch. "I *have* everything I want and will ever need, and her name is Savannah." He grabbed his cup and paper bag from the barista and walked out the café.

"You'll regret this, Andrew! She doesn't even love you. She can't love you. For all you know, she could be dead." Vanessa shouted after him, Andrew simply waving her off.

***

Months passed by, and Andrew never left his lover's side, replenishing her feeding tube and making sure she was as comfortable as she could be. There were times when Andrew felt lonely, wishing he had someone to talk to and hold him back, but he'd been down that road before, and he'd almost lost Savannah because of it. No, he couldn't do that to her again, not after what happened last time. Besides, there was still some hope in him that Savannah would wake up again. He hadn't given up yet. Until then, he would have to make due with knowing that, at least, she was still alive.

Every day became the same routine. Waking up for work in the morning and giving Savannah a kiss on the cheek before heading out the door. Coming home late at night and giving Savannah a kiss on the check before heading to bed. He'd stop going out with his friends and coworkers, choosing to spend time with Savannah instead.

He used to love going out, both of them, but most of the time, it was only because Savannah wanted to. It just wouldn't be the same without her. Every day was the same…until it wasn't.

One morning, Andrew felt a soft brush against his face and the whisper of his name in his ear.

"Andrew, Andrew."

He slowly opened his eyes and saw a blurry face staring back at him, blinking. Startled, he jumped out of bed, grabbed his bat, and started swinging.

"Take one more step near me, and I'll bash your head in."

"Andrew, stop! It's me, Savannah!"

Rubbing his eyes and squinting to take a closer look, Andrew saw the familiar face.

"Oh my god, Savannah!" He dropped the bat and ran over to the other side of the bed, hugging Savannah so tightly that he could feel a slightly hint of air escape her. "Pinch me, I must be dreaming."

"You're not. I love you, Andrew, with all my heart." Savannah hugged him back.

Andrew pulled slightly apart, so happy that tears welled in his eyes. "I thought I lost you forever," he cheered, as he leaned down to give her a kiss. "We truly are soulmates."

Chasing Soulmates

184